DEATH MASK

NIGHTVALE - BOOK II

RAZÖRFIST

Death Mask
Nightvale 2

RazörFist

Published by Dark Legion Books
Switzerland
www.arkhavencomics.com

Cover: Dominus
Illustrations: George Alexopoulos & RazörFist

ISBN: 978-952-7303-48-1

Contents

Kara'Zin

Dedicated to Fritz Leiber
The forgotten father of it all

Chapter 1
A Wraith Amid the Ruins

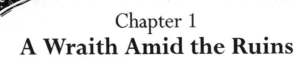

Trisday, 1st of Torgan
1856

The craggy-faced enforcer was quick. Just quick enough to cradle his intestines before they spilled from his piteous stomach but not quick enough to prevent it from happening.

The phantom was just merciful enough to cleave his head from his shoulders before he fully comprehended what was happening. The semi-circle of hired highwaymen could do nothing but gawk in horror as the beshadowed figure wiped his long, silver rapier clean of their comrade's entrails.

"Sh... Shirái..." one murmured in quavering terror.

The language was Izákás.

The word was a name.

It meant many things. Ghost. Spectre. Yet over weeks of whispering death, it had acquired a unique meaning in this desolate country.

"The Wraith."

DEATH MASK

None knew its origin. None dared divine its purpose. Only vague descriptions of a shrouded form, with obscured features, walking with an uneven gait, an argentine blade perpetually dangling at its side, ever thirsty for sinful blood. The hooded figure had appeared in the outer reaches of Vale over one month ago, leaving a trail of bisected criminal bodies, headless henchmen, and vanishing crimelords in its wake. After a moonlit tavern massacre in the twin capital of Tirionus, reports soon reached the west that it had been spotted crossing the Valen/Nazgani border near the peasant village of Romatho.

The corresponding blood-soaked siege of the city's underworld confirmed the hushed rumor. Inexorable and deliberate as death itself, the formless thing had cut through the criminal element of two countries before any reprisal could be mobilized. The cabals of Kara'Zin, the capital of Nazgan and veritable den of debauchery, had dispatched hired assassins to the easternmost reaches of the A'lidar Desert to quash the invisible assailant.

That they had already sent three parties ahead—none of whom had yet returned—failed to appear on the employment contract.

Beneath the billowing cloak, the Wraith suddenly and violently doubled, as with a light convulsion.

The sellswords hesitated, but only momentarily. Even their meager faculties did not fail to recognize an opportunity.

It was not until they neared for the kill that they at last calculated the enormity of their misstep. Bounding inhumanly from the feint, the Wraith lashed out with its one dangling arm at the nearest of the five. Slapping his sword point away and stabbing viciously through his dismantled guard, the swordpoint protruding from the back of the thug's neck punctuated the error more profoundly than any acrobatics on the swordsman's part.

Their blood afire, the remaining cutthroats did not falter.

Batting the first two aside, a dark-skinned, dagger-wielding murderer managed to break through and lash out with two blades at once. His knifepoints met nothing but the already-frayed edges of the revenant's cloak. For the Wraith had darted. Spun. Whirled.

Into a perfect pirouette that ended with a savage sideswipe.

His would-be killer fell in two pieces. He did not rise again.

A WRAITH AMID THE RUINS

A stocky Nazgani at his side swept upward at the vengeful spirit with a bulky broadsword. The Wraith's riposte and downward sword stroke ensured he would never wield a two-handed weapon again. The assassins' attacks came from all directions. The silver sword met them all.

With just two remaining men, the attackers at last ducked behind the rubble to regroup. There was no shortage of it. The westernmost outpost of Rináz had been immolated in more than one war in centuries past. After the fifth, they finally stopped rebuilding it.

The desert wind was picking up, but even over the low, desolate howl, they could hear a shuddering sigh at their back. The smaller swordsman's curiosity momentarily supplanted his fear, and he shot a glance over top.

Nothing.

The lethal shade, the cinereal cloak, the burnished, bloodstained blade, in a flash, all had diminished into ghastly remembrance. As the two crooks cowered among the rubble, a solitary whisper reverberated about the ruins. One scarcely even recognizable as a name.

"Xeeeerdessssssssss...."

Xerdes propped a leg against the wall, leaned back in his chair, and eyed his companion warily over a terracotta tankard of pallid ale. The squat, bulbous barkeep wrung his hands nervously against his filthy apron and attempted to tidy the dining arrangements before them. It was like dropping a daisy on a dung pile. The table looked like a fallen log he'd decided to make the best with, and taking a moment to consider the surroundings, Xerdes could see considerable expense had been spared.

The roof of the inn loomed low, wreathed in plumes of pipe smoke that reeled hypnotically in the air above its boisterous patrons, its midportion pregnant with the sodden earth above. Taverns of this sort were sheared into the soil like the sunken dwellings typical of this country, with the added benefit of providing more effective cooling in the harsh deserts of Nazgan.

Even in a city of secrets like Kara'Zin, the tavern held many.

Rogues leered from the shadows and plotted in sparsely lit corners, drunks reeled, and wenches fended off inebriate advances. A

"He was nothing anyone would look twice at. The second look told the story."

blind peasant child in an oversized fez begged for zalas[1] at the inner door. If dirty looks were currency, he'd leave with a wealthy inheritance.

The air hung thick with the scent of spice and filth. Though this was a city of the Bords, this particular tavern, situated as it was at the heart of the L'Intaza Alienage, was known for serving Men and other waylanders almost exclusively. Its middle-aged proprietor was perched on a squat little wooden stool, his bulging midsection spilling forth beneath a humble uniform. His hair was a carefully greased crop, pulled tight to the side, its black untamed curls still visible through the oil slick atop it. He was nothing anyone would look twice at.

The second look told the story.

"Xerdes, is it?" the barkeep inquired, all but hiding behind his wafer-thin mustache.

"Correct," the thief replied. The tavernkeep started to speak. His companion cut him off with a wearied eyeroll. "...You will now ask why my name is Nazgani in origin."

The barkeep was dumbstruck but steadied himself enough to dislodge a response. "I... I had... that is, I perhaps had begun to wonder—"

"...and I will reply that 'it's a long story', and you, being the type to pry using liquor as lubricant, will press the issue..."

Xerdes drank deeply of the mug of ale and with a wince, continued.

"...at which point, we will be at an impasse. Let's just say 'my story starts here' and let the matter rest while you find further reasons *not* to explain why you requested my services. In Kara'Zin, you're not exactly lacking for options..." he finished, indicating with a wave of the hand his patronage of cutpurses and cutthroats arrayed about the establishment.

Thieves predominated in Nazgan's capital.

It was a city marooned by the empires of men, bones of their legions long consigned to the whirling winds of the A'lidar Desert in a failed attempt to reclaim it. In the absence of order, one was created where predator preyed on predator, where legalized cartels clashed with coteries of thieves in the all-too-brief evenings, and where the knotwork hierarchy of disparate guilds yielded an empire of perfidy. Even the

---

[1] **Zalas:** Nazgan coin comes in three denominations. The zala, or tin, is the least of these.

Sálár—though officially recognized as the sovereign ruler of Nazgan—
was little more than the long-ascendant Queen of Thieves. Her ancestor
was still quietly called the Royal Usurper.

Very quietly.

The barkeep's composure crumbled.

"I w-will give you all the reward I can spare, sir!" he suddenly sobbed.
"My b-beloved is gone. My *Sháiná*! I fear terribly for her safety."

With a furtive glance over his shoulder, Xerdes leaned closer.

"Best to turn the cards over now, I think," he said, softening his tone.

The barkeep wiped his eyes and reassembled himself. There was plenty
to reassemble.

"I was not always the shambles you see before you, sir."

Xerdes leaned his shoulder against the low back of his chair and replied,
"The thought had occurred to me." With that, his index finger fell against
a thick gold ring adorning one of the innkeep's sausage-like digits. It had
a unique quality. Richly inlaid with winding black tendrils carven into its
aurous surface, at its center gleamed a single emerald, smoothed round as
a hen's egg into a solitary, eye-catching protuberance. It caught Xerdes's
eye more than most.

Contrasting the squalor of their surroundings against the gaudy trinket,
Xerdes took it to be the lone lingering glimmer of pride a long-humbled
man had afforded himself.

"I... once belonged to the L'Intaza, sir."

Xerdes shook his head incredulously.

"Always knew I was destined to break bread with nobility."

"I assume you know the story then. The Bords[2]... have long resented
our presence."

"...like a descending foot resents a bug."

"Too true. The Calamity gave them their excuse," the inkeep continued, "Seermen of the Zi'Zin Temple had long prophesied we would
cause doom. Finally, we were blamed even for the shaking of the Earth.
We were divested. Our lands seized or simply razed. I was luckier than
some."

---

[2] **Bords:** The residents of the deserts of Nazgan. Reptilian, lanky, and apelike in
   stature, they are known for their craftiness, religious piety, political upheavals, and
   inherent distrust of waylanders.

The thief took another lingering look at their drab surroundings. He said nothing.

"...My lands were seized on *paper*, but... in practice, my estate was so distant from the nearest settlement, not even the tax collectors would trouble themselves to send a garrison. And so I remained. A blade above my head."

Xerdes watched the man's eyes widen three sizes and well with nascent tears.

"...and then I met *her*," the barkeep added. "My Sháiná. My desert ro—"

"I've had too much ale to stomach the wedding story. I gather she's been... taken?"

"I know not," the barman replied in a voice the size of a pebble. "Since my reversals, she has... come and go at times."

"Some women are just looking for a reason to go missing," Xerdes mused aloud.

"Wherever she might be, if you consent, I suggest you start your search at my estate. She has... many reasons to revisit it."

"Some more sentimental than others, I wager," Xerdes chuckled, "Maybe even a few locked up behind a thick vault door? Requiring the service of an intrepid young safecracker rather than one of your regulars? That about the size of it?"

The barkeep's eyes hit the floor with shame. He started to speak, but the thief adjoined his previous statement instead, "Can I assume I'm being paid in more than sad looks and liquor?"

Morosely, the man made for his coinpurse. His very *light* coinpurse.

"Whatever I once was... *today*, I am a tavernkeep. I can offer but a humble stipend."

"How humble?"

"50 zalas at most."

"...and I had such high hopes for this conversation." Xerdes said with a shrug. Downing the remainder of his drink, he turned to leave. The frantic innkeeper intervened. With a speed he shouldn't have possessed, all at once his ruddy corpulence barred the path like a boulder in a rain gutter.

"I beg you reconsider, sir."

"Look, pal. There's humble, and then there's self-hatred."

"I... I may not be moneyed, sir," he stammered, "But the mansion is a loss, Sir Thief. One I've written off, regardless. You're welcome to keep the entire contents of the strong room as payment."

The edge of the thief's mouth pulled into a smirk.

"You had your openers and closers reversed."

"May... mayhap it has been raided by other thieves, but... in that remote location? I think not. You will find it quite unspoiled, I think. Though, in the long years, I... I fear I no longer possess the key..."

The innkeeper paused, and the grin that unspooled itself across his craggy features did his face no favors.

"...not that this will be a problem for you."

"What good is it to her then?" Xerdes asked, turning his eyes away from the man's corn-colored teeth.

"She... may not be alone," the barkeep admitted, shoulders sagging with invisible strain. "More men than you can penetrate a vault in this godless country."

"So long as we're pretending that's all he's penetrating," Xerdes jibed, almost unbidden, aided in no small part by the ale.

The barkeep weathered the quip in silence.

"I... I am Azin," began the barman, extending a meaty paw. Xerdes shook it once and coldly. "I should... warn you. My estate. The location is not the only reason garrisons have avoided it. It has acquired a reputation."

"...and with my luck, I'm betting it's not as a brothel."

Azin choked back a nervous laugh and continued, "To be expected, I suppose. It is a strange and eerie country. It lies between here and Tralini. In the heart of the Whispering Waste."

Xerdes' eyes narrowed. His face noticeably whitened, but his features stood unfazed beneath the low-slung hood. He knew the place exactly. And the odious reputation that came along with it.

"I have every faith in your abilities. You are, as I hear it, a *master*."

The thief gathered up the meager collection of coins, spun on his back heel, pulled his cloak from the back of his chair, and made for the door.

As he passed the blind beggar child, he dropped a coin into his fez and muttered to himself.

"...at everything but making a living."

Chapter 2
Blood on the Wind

Creaday, 2nd of Torgan
1856

Expeditious gusts of stinging sand lashed at the thief's cloaked frame as he stumbled through the searing deserts of Nazgan. Resolute eyes peered out into the darkening distance. Naught but arid, eyeless horizon stretched for miles in every direction. Sand as smooth as silken finery, battered prostrate by winds as perilous as an ocean torrent, promised anonymous death at every turn.

Fate had beckoned him back to this dark and desolate country. Nazgan. His home away from Hell. The cutpurse capital of the western world and one of the few havens for a hoodlum so outcast amongst his own. He knew well the names by which it was known. The Bloodied Sands. The Dunes of Death. The Menuvian underworld had its own name for it: "The Big Nothing."

A silvery mirage pursued by generations of Men, occasionally even attained, but never long held.

The land where the imperial legions had marched off to die, and their king had let them do it.

Here he shuffled, heeding the dubious advice of a phantom informant, to the utmost outskirts of the high desert in search of an abandoned citadel reputed to be buried somewhere between Kara'Zin and Tralini among the shifting sands of the A'lidar badlands. A forsaken fortress, given back to this inhospitable hellscape during the Cataclysm of 1850. Known in the Bords' obscure tongue by the ominous name *Nát'In*[1]. He'd learned the hard way why the Bords had taken to calling these badlands "The Whispering Waste." The atmosphere made a blast furnace sound frigid, and the wind was just quiet enough to hear a volcanic eruption.

---

[1] **Nát'In:** "The Dead Castle" or "Castle of the Dead," depending on the degree of poetic license one employs with the Bord language.

15

Ancient explorers had chained guideposts in the sand every seventy paces or so, long since consigned to the unceasing haboob. Every so often, Xerdes could have sworn he heard faintly distinguishable voices on the air. Whispers and enigmatic susurrations among the deafening roar of the sighing sands. Rather than doubt his sanity, Xerdes put it down to thirst and his thirteen-hour journey.

Even the Horrands, whose wintery homeland and distrust of the Bords rarely led them to these desolate tracts, had encountered the phenomenon, and assigned it an appropriate nomenclature.

"Gûntäug."

The Ghostwind.

It was not uncommon for a hapless traveler to hear the voice of a departed relation in that hissing soundscape or to spy the phantom of a forgotten flame in its roiling depths. Some were even said to have seen soldiers, still uniformed, flesh long decayed from skeletal bodies, that had perished in the long religious wars between the L'Intáza dominion of Men and the newly ascendant Sálas of the Bords, who had skulked out of the desert as refugees centuries prior and slowly, quietly conquered their kingdom in 1817. The fields of A'lidar were sown with the blood of Bords and Men.

Suddenly, a cyclonic gust whipped Xerdes's reeling body so hard that he nearly cartwheeled down the slope of a dune to his immediate left. High leather boots buried themselves deeply in the more stable sands beneath, just bracing his body low enough to avoid a compulsory plummet. His once-drawn hood had all but unfurled into a scarf, half-strangling him as it waved in a mad blur at his back. Short, unruly tufts of hair had long since become a brown bramble encrusted by the sandy spray. Even the stern eyebrows perched above his deeply set brown eyes and three-day growth of beard were nearly spackled with soil. A full day beneath the smoldering orb of Wytón[2] had somehow done little to darken the ivory pallor the thief had earned through uncountable evenings of moonlight larceny. He looked like half-baked bread: pale but browning at the edges.

Through the thickening, sodden spray, Xerdes could no longer distinguish the direction of his advance. Even casting his eyes upward

---

[2] **Wytón:** Valen name for the sun, from the Aven word for 'Light'. This is reductive, however. In the Aven tongue, 'Light' is a synonym for 'Creation' or 'Birth'.

yielded only the certain knowledge that something luminous loomed overhead. It wasn't globular or even distinct. But it certainly lit the billowing sandspray up just clearly enough to prevent vision in all directions. In that moment, the thief understood why the Bords had once worshiped the sun itself as divine. The tempest intensified, pulling Xerdes's right foot from its planting place. With a creaking lash, his lambskin flask was torn violently from his belt and hurtled sidewise, disappearing into the arenaceous ether. He'd have minded it more if he hadn't emptied it of water two hours previous. For the past half hour, there had been more sandstone in his parched palette than on the Earth itself.

Xerdes required concealment in the wake of the Long Moonlight. Now he had it. Ironically, it appeared the Whispering Waste would be hiding his corpse.

Then he heard it. More than a mere whisper. A voice. Suspended in the turbid heart of this barren blizzard.

"Jáhár'Nát!" it whispered. Then repeated. And repeated.

"Jáhár'Nát!"

Soon, it was booming in his ears like drums in the desert mists until he could no longer discern whether it emanated from the deadly sandsquall... or reverberated within his own skull.

"Jáhár'Nát!"

The whisper became a scream.

Then, soaring through the windswept desolation, the corner of his eye caught an object. Muscles tensed, wrenched his curved dagger free of its scabbard, and batted the mysterious missile away with the practiced reflexes of a wild feline. As the projectile catapulted impotently into the gale, he recognized it as a throwing knife with a two-pronged hook on either side. A length of cord was fixed to its looped tail. A necessity in these windswept wastes. No sooner had it struck the ground than it was drawn back into the flurry by his unseen assailant.

He knew before they brought blades to bear exactly their identity.

Xerdes had secured his tip in a tavern for a reason: Kara'Zin was a thieves' paradise. Provided you belonged to one of the many guilds in the decaying desert metropolis. Back home, thievery had been a vocation. In Nazgan, it was a way of life. So long as regular tribute was paid to the foremost among them: the Afa.

Thievery and assassination were legal in Nazgan. As much as being regulated and taxed makes anything legal. After centuries spent cowering in alleys and hideaways, cutting throats to preserve their secrets, the removal of the L'Intaza had facilitated the Afa's ascent to the highest halls of the Salar's government, taking their place alongside the Mi'Mhád merchant guilds, Zi'Zin Temple, Jeh'Mhár nobility and the throne of the Salár herself, as one of the five immovable pillars of Kara'Zin governance. Thus appointed to lord over the underlings, the Afa now demanded the selfsame suzerainty of waylanders that they imposed upon their native cutpurses.

As such, independents were discouraged and then discouraged at the end of a knife blade. Xerdes was intimately acquainted with both.

Stooped forms took shape in the scourging sandstorm. Indistinct figures which appeared doubled over and apelike. Long, lanky forearms propped up truncated hindquarters. As they stepped through the desolate din, he could clearly discern they were Bords.

Skins of varying veridian shades, some baked by the sun to darker expressions of brownish green, each inch of unrobed flesh bristling with reptilian scales on their exposed skin. From beneath drawn hoods and headwraps, darksome, inscrutable slits served for eyes.

The Afa had come to collect their tribute.

Xerdes grasped the hilt of his only currency.

"Iká!," he heard a hooded Bord hiss at his side, as the ambuscade pressed in. The serpentine blade protruding from his long, gauntleted right arm said more than the alien tongue ever could. In his few dealings with the reptilian race, he'd noted their foreign fashion tended to emphasize their abnormalities rather than camouflage them. It made exactly one thing they didn't deliberately conceal.

Obsidian eyes like orbs of oil slid sidewise through narrowed sockets as they spoke. He struggled vainly to discern the meaning from their demeanor.

"Dán'zílá ír tsedá!" one of the Bords vomited at his back.

"Still easier to understand than some accents back home..." he stalled, momentarily pretending that he had one.

Xerdes found he was no more fluent in Bord body language. Halting, stiff, and sudden in their movements, piercing their veil of ophidian calm was all but impossible.

BLOOD ON THE WIND

The stabwound he suddenly felt in his side ended the ambiguity. The Afa assassin had embedded a blade between his middle ribs. Xerdes pulled back, whirled, and in a single downward slice, the Bord's hand and forearm parted company. Black blood fired in fountainous abandon, showering his enemies in all directions as he fell with a piercing shriek. Xerdes tugged the Bord's blade free from his side and brandished it in his other arm. Two-fisted knifeplay was far from the thief's usual method of combat, but he'd trained enough to perform in a pinch. Nine enemies remained, but most were still wiping their compatriot's plasma from their eyes.

Xerdes struck.

With a headlong dive, he leaped upon a nearby assassin still clearing Bord blood from his vision. This one was lankier than the others and enshrouded entirely in earthen robes. Xerdes dyed them black with Bord blood, pinning him to the dunes and stabbing viciously with both daggerpoints until his squeals were swallowed by the sandstorm. A fell whisper on the wind punctuated his demise.

A larger one wielded a spear to his left. Xerdes kicked the pikepoint down and pinned it in the sand. Using the shaft as a ramp, he catapulted himself daggerpoint first and embedded his blade in his throat. The dastard died with a single, sustained gurgle. A throwing knife hurtled through the whirlwind, bound for his back. Xerdes scarcely had enough time to duck, take firm grasp of the cord tied to its tail, and whirl it back in his enemy's direction. So merciless was the stroke that it splayed two Bords' throats open as they stood side by side. The sands were stained with ebon blood as they doubled over, slid down a dune, and died before reaching the bottom. The enemy that had launched it growled a curse and, with two of his robed compatriots, rushed his human quarry with swarthy blades pressed forward.

In observance of his long-held tradition of honorable combat, Xerdes reached deep in the dune at his feet and launched a fistful of sand in his attackers' dark, glassy eyes. They stumbled in unison with a hiss, the one on the left tripping haplessly over the middle murderer while the third tumbled backward down the edge of a dune and writhed in a heap. Xerdes slid at his reeling enemies, embedding both blades through the throats of the two that still stood, tasting the bitterness of Bord blood flowing down on him as he did so. The panicked thief was gasping for air

19

"Xerdes found he was no more fluent in Bord body language."

after his sustained assault, and the act of rising to his feet was anything but agile. He fell back into the ever-intensifying storm and let the savage winds lift him to his feet. The third enemy struggled up the side of the dune and swung his sword in a deadly diagonal arc. Xerdes avoided it by a hair's breadth. The thief spun, both blades at the ready. The whispering winds wailed in his ears.

Xerdes blocked a lateral slash with one blade and buried the other between the Bord swordsman's shoulderblades. A vile spew of atramentous fluid fired in all directions. He died with an oath to his heathen god on his reptilian tongue. Consumed by sheer blood fury, Xerdes' subsequent stab wounds were anything but necessary and anything but merciful.

Nor was the Bord bolt that soon sank into his left shoulder, piercing the thin leather chestplate that protected it with ease. The two remaining enemies had forsaken their swords for crossbows. The dagger he had purloined from a now-armless adversary suddenly slumped from a left hand that now dangled limp and powerless at Xerdes's side. The thief sank to his left knee, pangs of agony coruscating like lightning down his body. In that moment, where mortality seemed certain, he spoke no supplications to deities deceased, slumbering or otherwise. Xerdes had lived a wicked life. He would not profane the name of Anái now by entreating him for unearned clemency. As if in response to his unspoken appeal, the sands began to shift.

The whispers on the wind were a thunderous bellow now, and Xerdes felt every granule vibrating beneath his boots.

A massive, sable-skinned, slithering devilry reared itself through the sandswept haze. With an infernal bellow, it immobilized all three men so that before either Bord could turn to avoid it, its colossal, jag-toothed maw ripped through the sirocco like a lethal battering ram with such blinding brutality that their legs and feet remained fixed to the spot, even as their bodies were devoured in the darkening fume. Xerdes was showered in Bord blood and rivulets of reptilian flesh as the black blur swept past him. An ancient horror. A demon-reared leviathan of the oceans of old, stranded in the sands of A'lidar by arcane calamity. As their screams carried on the harrowing winds, his mind only began to process the gape-jawed spectre that had seized them.

Idle tavern tales had become real before his astonished eyes.

The Whispering Windserpents of Nazgan.

21

DEATH MASK

With the black blizzard already calming itself in their wake, Xerdes did not tarry in returning to his tired feet, nor did he loot the bodies of the Afa assassins. He bent to remove a single enemy bow and quiver of arrows from the earth and fled in a flurry of dust, moving in the northerly direction of his goal.

The lonely mansion swallowed by the sands of A'lidar beckoned.

Nát'In.

The Dead Citadel.

His sand-blind eyes affixed on earthly wealth and one wayward woman, Xerdes answered its deathly summons.

Even the most frigid tracts of the A'lidar night could not be stilled. The Ghost Wind thundered across the blood-caked earth with merciless purpose. Mere hours after their encounter with the waylander from Menuvia, the bodies of his would-be Afa assassins were already half submerged by the unrelenting sandswell.

A black shape sprawled across the moonlit dunes, steadily encroaching upon the cadaverous site. It paused mechanically, seeming to silently consider the import of the Bord corpses strewn about it. A bracing gust made its tattered cloak billow beneath the silvery sky, and for but a moment, one might have distinguished it as the cloaked form of a man. One bent, asymmetrical, looming weirdly to one side, and steeped in inky silhouette.

Furtively, the dark form coiled to the earth to survey the bodily wreckage. From beneath the fluttering cloak, a ragged, heavily wrapped limb stretched to caress the dead flesh before it. Lithe digits probed for meaning, lingered pensively, and at last receded into the inky mass.

Then the shrouded penumbra jerked violently to the left, its hooded head noting faint impressions of bootprints, blown all but smooth in the ceaseless gale.

Then the thing rose like a living shade, seeming at once to lurch forward, in an uneven gait at once awkward and balletic, seeming to flow from dune to dune.

The Wraith then disappeared over the horizon, only the faintest, hissing whisper trailing in its unearthly wake.

Chapter 3
The Dead Citadel

Fallday, 3rd of Torgan
1856

By the time he had traversed the final dune, Xerdes's tongue had more grain than the desert. An eerie afternoon stillness had settled on the sandswept plain upon which a forlorn fortress ascended, silent and inviting, yet somehow unreal. The edifice was weirdly untouched by the blustery gales of the A'lidar Desert. All was white stone and maroon paint on masonry. A lone alabaster spire sprawled to the heavens at its center, its impeccably polished brass dome coming to a perfect curvature at its apex. A prodigious, semicircular archway was cast wide before a burnished stone bridge that spanned precisely nothing. Its unspoiled allure beckoned the thief to shoulder his suspicions and enter.

Yet as he neared the windswept citadel, the idyllic environ turned ominous. For as he cautiously crept through the enormous entranceway, a spectral sight bewitched his vision. All about him, in every verdant courtyard, below the causeway, even below his very feet, was a queer, shallow expanse of water that stretched in all directions. At first, he harbored the mistaken suspicion that a fountain had overflowed, but as he penetrated the innermost depths of the estate, it became inescapably obvious that he had found the entire property flooded in nearly a full foot of ground water.

In mounting bewilderment, he inspected the fluid closely and found it to be utterly transparent and unpolluted. Without question, it was water from an underground spring.

Xerdes's arid throat overcame his momentary caution. He fell to his knees, cupped trembling hands into the pool, and drank deeply. Even under the oppressive sun, it was frigid with a deathly chill. Within seconds, it had satiated the thief's thirst enough that he cringed, as if only now aware of his copious, if superficial, wounds.

"The edifice was weirdly untouched by the blustery gales of the A'lidar desert."

THE DEAD CITADEL

He stood nevertheless replenished, feeling the blood pulsate through reinvigorated veins.

With no flask to refill, he instead took in his bizarre surroundings. Tall towers spiraled to the sky above his head. If Sháiná was here, she had invented a new kind of quiet. A soft wind began to buffet his body, casting calm ripples across the face of the bizarre pond that stretched in all directions. He thought he caught sight of a strange shape beneath the babbling surface, yet when he turned to examine it, it disappeared.

Xerdes felt the water soaking through the soles of his boots as he aimlessly meandered around the complex. It seemed unlikely anything more than metal valuables had survived this peculiar deluge, but the upper floors of the fortress doubtless held more. If the stories he'd heard in Kara'Zin held true, the grounds had rested, untouched by sand or siege, for years. Along with its wealth. He rewrapped his hood and drew it low over sunscorched eyes. Untouched or not, he preferred to remain unseen.

It was only upon stepping through a rounded doorway leading into the antechamber of the citadel itself that he at last comprehended the extent of the mystifying flood. Even indoors, he stood in a foot of water at least. Roiling reflections against frescoes of the mythic past were scrawled across the high ornate ceilings, bearing haunting testament to the once-noble keep's aquatic repose. The Bords and Nazgani nobility had an abiding affection for tactless ornamentation, and Nat'In did not differ in this regard. Silver serpents coiled their carven way up stalwart pillars to touch the ceiling, which stood stoic and remote overhead.

The combination of the reverberant building and irrigation at his feet made traversal alarmingly unsilent. Even the most controlled, practiced advance sounded like a sailing skiff sinking to the depths of the Cerulean Gulf.

For a fleeting moment, he heard a faint bellow from beneath it. He paused.

Nothing but distant dripping sounds from an adjoining chamber met his ears.

The sound had ceased the second he stopped.

Xerdes pressed on, his heart thumping harder than he would have preferred.

A long, wide hallway yawned before him, with bulbous pillars positioned at regular intervals. A plush carpet of sanguine red, now stained green by lichen in the intervening half decade of abandonment stretched from his feet, while the overhead banners bearing cursive Izákas script began to billow in a light breeze that spilled in from glassless windows, echoing the carpet's intended color. The windows were little more than emaciated slits, allowing sickly shafts of waning sunlight to cast feeble illumination on the interior of the watery cave.

A sudden vibration cracked the marblework at his feet. Xerdes nearly tumbled into the unnatural lagoon but steadied himself on a nearby pillar. As he looked on in bafflement, the pool began to bubble and froth about his legs. From deep beneath the surface, beyond the marble tiles of the floor itself, a dizzying kaleidoscopic floodlight illuminated the gloom. Shafts of blinding yellows, icy blues, and rich and dazzling magentas combed the surface of the water from below, as if peering out into the landed world above. The thief's mind reeled. For in that instant, Xerdes could scarcely discern which world was above or below.

Desert wind shrieked through the thin window slits such much that Xerdes had to hold his hood down with one hand to preclude its removal.

Marshaling the utmost masculine fortitude, he daintily leaned forward and cowered before the ageless fathoms below. The light's glare was so extraordinary that it nearly whitened his sight, but as he relaxed his eyes and pulled ever closer to the boiling basin, he began to distinguish abyssal shapes in the darksome deep. For a single, heart-rending moment, he clearly recognized one as a human skull.

A terrific concussion ended the watery reverie.

Like a cannonball crushing against ocean waves, a terrific spray shot to the ceiling, knocking the awestruck thief against the far wall and treating him to a deep, bracing gulp of groundwater in the bargain.

A coiling, sepulchral shadow of massive stature reared itself before him. Its scaled, serpentine mass gleamed in the darkness.

Like a lock yielding to the thief's unerring skill, the final tumbler clicked into place.

The water.

The wind.

He had located the abode of the Whispering Windserpents of Nazgan. This was no mansion. It was a nest. At this precise moment, he stood in a basilisk brooding ground.

"Vilnia's *tits*!" he spat and fumbled with the shortbow at his back. The slithering goliath sweated archaic evil. Water spilled from its ancient back, and steam rose in fetid plumes about its body. The creature dwarfed every marble column, including the one Xerdes crouched behind for imagined protection as he hastily nocked an arrow to his weapon and cursed his ill fortune. Hatred spilled from its jagged maw, a crag-toothed grin mocking him in the darkling gloom.

"The vault!" An unfamiliar voice suddenly shrieked through the murk. "Make for the vault!"

Xerdes followed the voice. A gargantuan, recurved doorway dominated the opposite end of the hall. Its entire circumference fastened to the wall with 4 broad iron beams which latched in a cross pattern from opposing directions. The blocky, cursive script of Izákás skirted its entire perimeter. He could not be certain, but it seemed to throb faintly. Whether it was some manner of magical ward or another trick of the light, he hadn't time to discern. Below the door, languid against the edge of a dais leading up to the vault, was the sprawled form of a woman. Her exit was blocked by the beast.

Xerdes turned to fire an arrow at the monstrosity. It struck hard at its scaled side and catapulted harmlessly into the watery mire with a splash. A low, demonic bellow shook the rafters, then. Breathless with terror, Xerdes heard it emanate from the very walls about him. He soon realized it had emerged from the creature itself. A green, viscous sputum shot from between the Windserpent's knife-edged teeth like a surf over the jagged rocks of a waterfall.

Xerdes cursed again and cartwheeled behind another ornamentally adorned pillar. Hands shaking violently, he managed to withdraw another arrow and nestle it tight against his bowstring. Something struck the column so hard it threw the thief to his knees. Spinning to see what it was, Xerdes did so just in time to witness the very same pillar lurching toward him. Preparing to topple.

As the support collapsed upon him, he thought he heard a woman's shriek. A blinding blue-green glow emanated from all around him. He felt the earth cast wide beneath him and feared a fatal plummet.

Then the world was subsumed by blackness.

Chapter 4
Negotiation at Knifepoint

Maeday, 4th of Torgan
1856

A wall stood stoic before him.

It was a perfectly smooth thing. Flat, broad matte black, for no light's sheen escaped its surface. A gray ethereal expanse of sensation and memory spanned in all directions, but the barrier prevailed even among the swirling nothingness.

He stood transfixed by the bizarre barricade. Its perfect constancy seemed an affront to the amorphous fogworld in which he found himself adrift.

And then he felt his arm reaching out for it. His bare hand stretching. Probing. Touching the perfectly smooth surface.

In that moment, he became cognizant that he was not approaching the bulwark with feet firmly planted. He was floating. Falling. The barrier became a hole. He hurtled headlong into its black heart.

His fingers touched the surface of it. No solid substance met them. A wordless terror clawing its way to his throat, he found himself cartwheeling into an obsidian void. He had merged with the mortal dread.

Xerdes catapulted headlong through the other side of the stygian wall, sputtering liquid shadow. It coursed down his leather breastplate, staining his skin. He hacked violently and attempted to sit erect while he gathered his wind.

A hand he could have worn as a hat sat him back down.

"Easy, friend," he heard a deep voice with a Göurnoth accent say. "You've some time yet to fully recover."

"...the catnip blooms in winter," he heard himself say. It was someone else's voice, but his Xerdes impersonation was spot on.

"He was under too long, Kev," a woman's voice soothed. "Could there be permanent damage?"

DEATH MASK

The thief's bottom eyelid fell like a slab of sheet rock as inky tendrils trilled across his vision. His mind began to gradually unfog itself, but his cryptic companions still seemed strange and ethereal before him. Even in a thick fog, he could have discerned the man was massive. At night. In a rainstorm. Strawberry b locks catapulted down a domed forehead that might, at a passing glance, have seemed adequate housing for a brain. They spilled down two perfect right angles some might have confused with shoulders. A beige tunic clung fast to his athletic physique, and dangling from a leather thong about his neck were runic charms in the ancient language of Agrigör. Either a human of Horrand ancestry, or someone pretending to such. He was either built for battle or bedrooms.

The woman seemed as if she had seen her fair share. Two deep viridian eyes, impossibly remote and steeped in sin, peered wildly from behind a dark contoured face framed by a painstakingly erected braided bun of hair pulled behind with two steel pins in the style characteristic of the region, her lips red to the brink of blackness, as if she'd only now alighted the theater stage. Her voluptuous form was constrained by sensuous purple garments. Xerdes could see enough to know they were insufficient to the task.

Sháiná

Through blinkered vision, he stared at her. She warranted a stare.

"Xerdes," she said, in a smoky lilt that pleased his body more than his brain. "Are you still with us?"

He sat up. It was a good start.

"Do you read fortunes?" Xerdes grumbled.

Her eyelashes fluttered. It was a practiced gesture. He couldn't decide which was more fake.

"...plucking my name from the clear blue sky, I mean."

She shot a sideways glance at the big man. Xerdes caught it before he did.

"You were... moaning while you were out," the man fumbled. The explanation had a certain understated stupidity.

"We... even conversed a bit," the brunette said, salvaging the brute's witless gambit, "You were out of it for nearly a day. I'm..."

"...Sháiná." Xerdes cut her off with a wince as he sat up further.

"Your..." The thief looked her up and down. He didn't rush. "...other half. Azin. He treated me to an ale."

The mist in his mind had dissipated so that his conversation partners very nearly looked human.

He heard the big one let loose a scoff that sounded like a thirsty horse at a water trough. He was as subtle as he was short.

"Kevelin," boomed the big man and extended a leather-braced forearm. The incredulous look he gave the giant as he let his hand hang awkwardly was Xerdes's answer to the scoff. He didn't know how much they knew. He didn't know how much *he* knew. What Xerdes did know is they weren't being honest. He decided to do likewise, if only to keep with fashion.

"I was hired to find you. Seems now you may not have been lost."

She shot him a look that he felt slide between his ribs. The wind picked up with a howl, punctuating the gesture.

"Men," she sneered. "All the same."

"So are women. Once you've known enough."

If she could have spat fire, he'd have been a lump of coal. She abruptly repossessed herself. Folding her hands on her lap and injecting just enough saccharine into her voice to prove she was entirely disingenuous.

"High words for a man we fished from his deathbed."

"I wouldn't call *anything* high in his company," Xerdes said, giving a thoughtless shrug in the oaf's direction. Kevelin almost understood enough to scowl. "But when the answers aren't straight, the story's usually crooked."

Bolts of ice beamed from green eyes. After a pause, she rejoined, "I left. Is that straight enough? Shall I discuss Azin's other shortcomings in detail?"

Xerdes struggled to his feet. His wavering legs had other ideas, but he steadied himself on Sháiná's shoulder and performed a fine approximation of standing upright. From the corner of his vision, he caught an acid glance from Kevelin. With something more. A dull glow. Something ghostlike. Horrid. As he turned to spot it, the man's eyes seemed at once perfectly normal.

For all his lumbering dullardry, Xerdes decided there was something ominous and remote about the man. Something not born of this plane. Something from the world's long-dead past.

Then he decided that was too much to get out of a single look.

"It'll keep the seat warm until the truth shows up," he said, turning back to Sháiná and incidentally, away from the eerie giant, "What's here for you then? Except an audience with a poison-spewing serpent."

"*Several* serpents. Actually." she shot back, "It's some sort of nest for the fell creatures now."

"I take it the pool is another recent renovation," He looked down at the foot of water around his shins in the courtyard splayed about them and noted, "Or was that the reason you and your husband left?"

"You say that as if I was old enough to remember," she said in a tone that could pulverize granite. Xerdes clicked his tongue against his teeth and shrugged.

"Is this not shocking where you are from, thief?"

She responded in disgust, in a manner that didn't quite fit her facial expression.

"What? That your engagement gift was a severed umbilical cord?" he scoffed, "I gave up surprise at the nobility's private perversions. Hard enough satisfying my own."

"Oh?" she purred. This time, the expression fit the face exactly.

He was working his way around to what it might have meant when he jolted upright.

NEGOTIATION AT KNIFEPOINT

The blade point that suddenly pressed itself against his back felt cool between his shoulder blades.

"Ah," sighed Xerdes, "I was wondering when we'd come to that."

"Don't be a hero, thief. There's no payday in it," warned the oaf.

"There haven't been many to date."

Kevelin brained him across the back of the head no harder than he would swat a fly. At his size, it was stiff enough to make the point. His vision momentarily doubled.

Sháiná's face flushed with arousal at the violent display. The wind was working up to a gale. It whined around the ivory pillars that circled the courtyard, gradually thickening with choking dust.

Her eyes devoured him.

"I have a task."

Xerdes chanced a look over his shoulder to the giant wedging a knifeblade into the middle of his back. The strange glow had left his steely eye.

"...and now I reckon it's mine, too."

Sháiná pulled tighter to him. Lavender carried on the wind that harrowed her bare, shapely back.

"Can a shared goal not be pleasurable?" he heard her ask, aware she wasn't really asking. The daggerpoint working its way to his spine told the thief that his male captor may not share her outlook on sharing.

"We do not need—" he heard the dullard start before Sháiná silenced him with a gesture.

"I ask only that you accomplish your original goal, Sir Thief," her honeyed voice soothed. "But... plunder my husband's strong room... *first.*"

"Sure. Let me ask the serpent to slither to another mansion oasis," he said with a wry chuckle.

"Have you come this far without slithering yourself? To weave with shadow? To fling wide the doors of the darkest, unknown vaults and... plunder their spoils in silence?"

"...the last bit I managed by not sloshing my way through a foot of water."

She was close enough to touch. He got the feeling the man with the dagger at his back wouldn't appreciate that. She took one venomous glance over Xerdes's shoulder and began to run her hands down his chest.

Kevelin seethed. He felt the daggerpoint twist.

"Who said anything about standing?" she replied, the contour of her lips sliding its way into a sensual smile.

"A coin, blaggard." He heard the big man offer, "You will fetch us a coin."

"Tyrions or Zalas?" mocked Xerdes. "Check my coinpouch. You can have just enough to need a whole lot more."

Kevelin wound around to Xerdes front and elbowed Sháiná to the side. Her eyes erupted in emerald fury.

"...I don't like your mouth," the oaf smoldered, his grip on the knife tightening perceptibly.

"That's all right. It's not on the market."

"It's not currency. it's a special item. Entirely of gold. And of excep-tional size," Sháiná cut Kevelin off with a brutal blow to the stomach, "Even among my husband's affluence... you will know it immediately."

"It will be silver. And *large*," her male companion added.

Xerdes's eyes narrowed as he craned his neck up at Kevelin, pondering how easily cowed the hulk had been by a female a fraction of his size.

Sháiná was either great on her back or terrible on her feet.

"Let's say you agree..." she started.

"Let's say I have a choice." Xerdes finished.

The goliath arm that suddenly clapped against his shoulder and the blade against his back verified the truth of that statement.

He was getting to be very fond of Kevelin.

Chapter 5
The Sálár Silverhawk

Maeday, 4th of Torgan
1856

The waters frothed and bubbled about their feet as the infiltrators stole once more into the mammoth corridor, as if the once-passive pool itself were disquieted by their intrusion. The waters themselves had warmed considerably. Whether from the fell serpents or whatever preternatural phenomenon had illuminated the natatorium previously, Xerdes devoted considerable effort to not speculating.

The thief felt Sháiná slither in behind him. Kevelin took audible exception to the gesture with a bellow befitting a hibernating bear. Xerdes couldn't decide if he was on the payroll or the menu.

The black shape rising from the steamy depths put a pause to the thought. He clung to his last breath like an acrophobic mountain climber. The melanoid mass slowly descended once again into the ghostly lagoon, a low, rumbling hiss punctuating its ebb.

The windserpents slumbered.

Daring to exhale, the thief beheld Kevelin, grinning in venal abandon. His eyes now locked upon the vault door opposite.

"I guess even riftspawn[1] have to sleep." he mused without blinking.

The hiss he heard next did not come from the serpent.

"Lose the smile, Kev. Your face looks better without it," Sháiná spat.

He traded it in for a scowl.

Xerdes couldn't see or even process the expression. All about him, it seemed an unearthly water threatened to envelop him. A hot spring of poisonous froth beckoned his plunge, and it was all he could do to look away. At the back of his mind, the black wall stood stoic.

---

[1] **Riftspawn:** A great fissure in the ground north of Highcrest known as The Rift (or Lithiolain) is believed to have unleashed hellish beasts upon the world of Travinas during the War of the Rift (929–985). Anything odd or unnatural can sometimes be colloquially referred to as Riftspawn.

"The Windserpents slumbered."

The thief was in no mood for a second encounter.

The pool no longer cast eerie verdigris reflections, but rather, a sea of spectral shapes seemed to glissade skyward, wavering in and out of the thief's vision. Clambering toward the ceiling in a single reptilian wave of revulsion.

"Whatever devilry is at work here," he whispered. "I'd rather see a windserpent's stomach from the *outside*."

"Oh, I doubt you'll be alive by the time that happens, pickpocket," rejoined Kevelin, the scowl still firmly in place. As if the blade at his back were too subtle an indicator of the death sentence that awaited him when they finally reached their objective.

Each slow, silent step through the knee-high bath became heavier with mounting dread. As Xerdes made to inch forward, he felt a massive paw pull him back abruptly. It was all the thief could manage not to catapult backward into oblivion.

He hurled a look at Kevelin that should have shorn his neck from his shoulders.

His captor stood stolid, the index finger on his right hand simply pointing downward. As Xerdes' vision followed to where it indicated, something moved in the water between his legs.

Something smooth. Something warm. Something that writhed about his ankles.

As his widening eyes followed the otherworldly wake, slowly the glistening hulk of a serpent's sleeping frame loomed into view, its slumbering mass still menacing from the shadows. Xerdes's foot had missed striking its tail by a gossamer's breadth.

It was no small wonder they slept at all, for the wind was a dusty gale, buffeting the structure at such speed it whistled through windows, doorframes, and even unsightly cracks in the edifice. It was near deafening, even indoors. The sound served to camouflage their approach.

"Perhaps you should have found a more surefooted safecracker, my dear," Kevelin scoffed at his back.

"I'll double my curtsey practice."

"Fate gives me a locked vault guarded by giant serpents? The gods send me a heavy-footed oaf and a half-smart harlequin," Sháiná muttered.

At length, he witnessed Kevelin nearly trip over the lip of a submerged dais and briefly fall to one knee.

Xerdes made sure he knew.

"No need to bow. Only one person here married into nobility. And it wasn't me."

"I'll rejoice in separating your spine fr—"

"SHH!" Sháiná interjected, "Look."

The three squinted in unison, for out of the murky phosphorescence, a circle of burnished gold glimmered at the edge of what they soon recognized as the elephantine door which barred passage to the Vaults of the Dead Citadel.

Xerdes wasted no time traversing the remaining distance, hands already feeling for his kit. Expert fingers withdrew three long-toothed picks as he bent before the titanic aperture and went to work. The mechanism was no puzzle, although three separate recesses, equal lengths apart beneath the four cross-shaped bolts he'd spied earlier, spanned the foot of the door. Presumably accepting a specially-fashioned key for each.

He went to work on the leftmost keyhole with the speed of a man possessed.

Long ago steeled against untold dangers, frigid fingers of fear nevertheless clawed at the back of the thief's mind. A prodigious task lay before him. Dormant demons slept in shallows of death at his back, a vault door at least equal to his abilities at his front, and his reward for accomplishing his task was a dagger to the throat and a second smile from his dusky captor and her barbarian paramour.

A dull click resounded in the hall.

Xerdes chanced a panicked glance over his shoulder.

For moments of breathless silence, all three intruders listened.

Only the steady, ragged intake of the land leviathans' breath as they dwelt in watery repose answered. The Ghostwinds that hammered the hall from the outside had deafened the windserpents entirely. Were they not standing nearly to their waists in water, Xerdes might have permitted himself to wonder if they could be roused at all. The unearthly tales of how the windserpents may never have dwelt in the deserts at all to begin with, but were catapulted here by the rising waters of the cataclysm, there to be stranded for eternity among Nazgan's shifting sands, silenced those thoughts. Whether they swam in sea or sand, he was in no hurry to test their sensitivity to the movement of water.

Xerdes gave a single twist of his head to Sháiná. She skulked hither inquisitively.

"Hold these picks in place," Xerdes commanded. "Don't let them move an inch."

The woman nodded with a devilish smile, taking peculiar enjoyment in his forceful tone.

He shot her a smirk of his own and reached for two additional picks.

The lock to the far right fell next, Xerdes being aware that these vault mechanisms usually required equal force applied on either side before the central lock would yield. The click of the lock acceding to his advances was all but inaudible over the wind outdoors. He indicated for Kevelin to hold said picks in place as well. This one agreed grudgingly. It was all he could do not to cringe as the clod's oxlike digits awkwardly clasped the picks.

Xerdes reached at his belt for two more.

His hand came away with only one.

"Adon's balls," he cursed beneath his breath. He'd exhausted his supply.

Cracking the lock with one pick wasn't a problem. Holding it in place was.

"Out of tricks already, blaggard?" he heard Kevelin chide to his right.

"Asking out of genuine curiosity or because you need professional guidance?" Xerdes said with a counterfeit smile.

"I thought you picked locks for a *living*," Kevelin responded in a tone like a falling boulder.

"I do an impression of a mute, too. See if you can do better."

Ignoring the thug's fumbling attempts to prod him, Xerdes's sharp eyes darted about the waterlogged chamber frantically. A faint reflection of pale aquamarine caught them to his immediate left.

Without sparing a second thought, the thief's hands reached over and plucked the hairpins that held Sháiná's impeccable coif in place. Sable ringlets lazily tumbled to her dusky shoulders, settling between her breasts. Xerdes spared her a glance. A long, healthy glance.

Just enough to elicit a throaty grunt from Kevelin.

The boxman went to work. It didn't yield willingly, but the work was quick all the same. Another dull click trumpeted his victory. There was something ominous beneath it.

DEATH MASK

A low, reverberating bellow seemed to emanate from all around him. To the ears of the terror-stricken thief, it was impossible to discern if it emitted from the barrier or beyond. Xerdes shook his head. His vision had gradually begun to narrow since entering the Windserpents' lair, likely owing to the oppressive air, but even his muddled faculties clearly discerned the maniacal sneer twisting its way across Kevelin's chiseled features.

With a sinister groan, the mammoth door began to yield inward. Impermeable blackness beckoned within. The silence was thick at Xerdes's back as he squinted into the inky depths of the vault before him.

"Afraid of an empty chamber?" his male captor mocked.

Xerdes's patience at last reached its end.

"I've been hard at work assuming you're only a conventional idiot. You're not helping."

Before the brute could blunder a reply, Sháiná intervened.

"He's right, Kev. For all we know, there's another nest back there."

Kevelin slowly withdrew, seething as he added, "Then how do we get what we came for and make sure we aren't interrupted by the current residents?" he said, indicating to the murky pool.

Xerdes drew an unlit torch from a brazier against the doorway, striking flint from his pouch until it at last lit.

"Simple. I go in. You stay here," he said, holding the torch high aloft, "...and pray they're heavy sleepers."

He turned back to the vault door, now looming half-agape before him. But not before he caught a sly look between Sháiná and Kevelin. As the thief stepped over the low lip of the circular doorway, he already pondered the glance. And knew precisely its import.

Once the coin was secured, his usefulness to his captors would be formally exhausted. There was only one play. Xerdes tried to keep that in mind.

It wasn't easy, given the sight before him.

It started with just a few coins, sprawled in a trail before the tips of his boots. Then rubies. Sapphires. Steely diamonds. The coins proliferated in number, until at last the trail led to a veritable canyon of aurous gold, piled in rolling hills against the far wall of the vault.. He could have sledded down the side and not seen the bottom until sunset. He thought about trying it, when another object caught his eye.

THE SÁLÁR SILVERHAWK

This one lay off to the side, in a more orderly, regimented antechamber, flanked by waist-high glass cases on either side. At their center, in a single transparent display, couched among black velvet, lay a series of smaller coins. Circling a single, massive object.

Kevelin had told him it would be a simple coin. Kevelin was an idiot.

The Sálár Silverhawk

It was a disc of polished sterling silver the size of a fist. Florid intaglios wound about its circumference, and painstakingly etched at its center was a vividly sculpted hawk, its talons clutching the standard of the Sálár of Nazgan. That they had nearly shredded the banner seemed to Xerdes a clever touch of the artist's own. For empires had been torn asunder for less in the harsh wastes where the Bords dwelt in isolation.

The case bore no lock. With a vault door that size, it didn't need one. He set his torch in a brazier on the wall beside him, lifted the lid in absolute silence, and bore it from its bed of black velvet. Into the waiting mouth of his waist pouch.

41

The thief regretted that he had but one further pouch to fill with wealth, but did so all the same, scooping several fistfuls of gold and rubies into the cloth expanse until the practical realities of marching home with a heavy belt made further theft inadvisable. He drew it shut and turned back toward the vault door, still yawning into the Windserpent's lair.

He stopped.

Kevelin stood there. Sháiná some distance back. Daggers drawn.

The victorious thief obediently stepped over the lip of the vault once more, abiding by Kevelin's wordless command. His head bowed in submission.

"I found no Silverhawk," he stalled.

Xerdes knew what awaited him.

There was no quieter fall guy than a dead man.

Which is why it seemed to make a marginal amount of sense when Xerdes paused, turned to the edge of the dais, looked to his captors one last time...

...and plunged face first into the waters before them.

A terrific splash shot high into the air, its sound seeming to shake the walls of the edifice itself.

Sháiná and Kevelin stood dumbstruck. Neither dared to breathe.

For many pregnant moments, they stood perfectly still, as if the Windserpents' sleep cycles hinged entirely on the amount of tension in their bodies.

And then they heard it.

It began as a slow, rolling rumble beneath their feet. Then the first splash received an emphatic reply. A terrific concussion spewed from the deathly mire, shifting the floor tiles beneath the intruders' feet. As they shuddered with wide-eyed terror, an umbral leviathan reared in the gloom, its roiling mass alight with unearthly luminescence. A putrid skull with frothing jaws agape, a high-pitched whisper emitting from its venomous maw, nearly struck the ceiling as it sprawled.

The Windserpents had awoken.

Kevelin spat a Horrand curse and used one muscular arm to scoop Sháiná hard against him, catching her off guard.

"He may not have found—it... but one of us will! All we need is a distraction."

Recovering from the sudden gesture, she whirled to look at Kevelin., who scooped down for a passionate kiss. The world seemed to pause in place until at last he tore himself away. Sháiná had scarcely regained her breath when she started. For Kevelin's face had suddenly contorted into a briar of mangled malevolence.

"You'll have to do," he whispered. And with one mighty arm, he flung her forward. Into the waiting jaws of the writhing Windserpents.

In a mad impulse, the barbarian spun toward the vault door, his unhinged cackling echoing throughout the expanse. His window would be brief, as one woman would only entertain the serpents for so long. He could all but taste the wealth that lay beyond. He had only started to step over the edge of the doorframe when a shadow fell before him. Unmanned, the Horrand thief craned his neck backward to learn the source.

Wide jaws sneered from the waiting darkness, and all at once, Kevelin knew. While he had stopped for a kiss, a serpentine shape had quietly coiled about them. He had unwittingly freed Sháiná from immediate danger.

And engineered his own death.

Despite his betrayal, Sháiná found herself choking back sobs on the pool's edge, even as Kevelin's screams, followed by the sound of sinew shredded from bone resounded in the watery corridor, the broiling pool beclouded in crimson.

"KEV!" she shrieked and in crazed anguish, started toward the door, when something leaped from the water and clasped her right ankle. The temptress prepared to unleash a horrified scream but was pulled under before a single sound could escape.

The waters stilled. All struggle, above the water and below, ceased.

Only the sickening sound of the ravenous basilisks gorging themselves on Horrand flesh predominated in the hellish hallway.

The far end of the watery chamber was all but silent. While the Windserpents fought with ever-increasing volume over their unexpected snack, the waters of the antechamber and the door leading inside were all but still.

All save one spot.

Just before the citadel's front door, two black shapes slithered toward the precipice and then all at once erupted across the threshold. The limp, soggy form of Xerdes gasped and crawled its way out the door to the outer garden beyond, with his quarry Sháiná dragged, unconscious, under his right arm. He coughed and spat, having ingested an improbable amount of water in his escape. The whispers on the wind had become a deafening roar. The thief's arms gave way, his shoulder collided with the earth, and all the world seemed enveloped in the howling winds of the A'lidar Desert.

Chapter 6
The Ghostwind

Time and Place Unknown
1856?

Xerdes found himself wandering in an ether of sand. There was no sky. No sun. No moon. Only the sensation of his booted feet being slowly swallowed by the pillowy mire gave the faintest impression there was earth beneath his feet. He had no conception of how he'd arrived at the eye of this whirlwind and no hint to the nature of the roaring desolation. The glassy winds stung the corners of his eyes and poured into his throat, and it was all he could do to hack clouds of the fine sand from his lungs.

Yet every aspect of the hellish vortex was dwarfed by the whispers. Remote at first. Then closing ever nearer. Until now, it was as if he'd cupped an ear to the lips of an intimate lover.

Peering haplessly into the gray, he could at first distinguish no names. No places.

Only disconsolate moans among the sounds of the wind.

Until a single word catapulted through oblivion.

Addressed to him.

"Trespasser..."

His squinting eyes bolted wide at once. For through the turbid hellscape, he caught a fleeting image directly ahead. A single skull. Bleached clean by the Nazgan sun. Atop its naked scalp tilted an iron helm, pitted by decades of neglect, despoiled by dust and decay. As the wraith emerged, closer than his most deathly imaginings, his ragged throat nearly croaked in alarm, but no sooner had it appeared than it receded once more into the wall of sheer opacity before him.

Even his sand-caked voice was able to exclaim aloud what he'd witnessed.

"The Ghostwinds of Nazgan..."

The whispers pitched dizzyingly upward in a stentorious crescendo. The effect was almost lyrical.

DEATH MASK

Xerdes realized at once he had stopped moving, his legs leaden to the sinksands about him. The winds had become so violent, his scarf seemed intent on garroting him. With a violent gesture, he wrenched it away from his shoulders. The fluttering fabric was so wholly swallowed by the sands, his vision scarcely caught it before it catapulted into the sedimentary void.

The corner of his eye barely caught the next phantom. Little more than amorphous movement at first, he seemingly had to whirl to his right to avoid colliding with it. The collision never occurred. For a skeletal spectre stopped before him, abruptly and now in perfect stillness. From the haggard frame, weathered flesh, stripped by aeons of dilapidation, draped in haggard rivulets of cloth and dessicated flesh like ivy from the ramparts of a despoiled citadel.

He knew its face.

"Xerdes..." it gurgled, drowning out the din.

Even worn away by seasons of rot, the face of his former friend and ally in thievery, Sia Tulune, was one he would always recognize. Even in life, he had the characteristic pallor of his people. Menuvians were known as much for their darkness of hair as for their fairness of skin. The chalk-white bone jutting through Sia's long-dead face could be described as anything but fair.

And then a lone word rumbled from the back of the dead, gaping maw.

"...betrayeeeerrrrrrrrrrrrrrrrrrr..."

Xerdes stood transfixed, an impotent reply dying on his tongue as the ghostwinds swallowed the phantom form, and it was swept away into the depths of the ether. His breath undone, the thief at last pressed onward into the vicious gale. Not two steps had he managed before another form took shape before his narrowed vision. Haggard. Rotted. Unmistakable.

A porous, half-moldering beard, brown and flecked with white, spilled from pursed, dilapidated lips. Xerdes gazed into the hollow sockets that had once held the eyes of his master and mentor, Wulf Eghenston. Twin streams of rusted crimson, caked dry by the merciless sun, flowed over furrows of fetid flesh. A keepsake from his Menuvian captors after the Wulf Pack had been sold out to the Menuvian guard. Eyes served as both ornament and instrument during the days-long interrogations favored by the Tower Guard, particularly for a career criminal like Wulf Eghenston.

46

Xerdes tried to speak, but only a whisper escaped his split, scorched lips.

The phantom did the speaking for both of them.

"My... chiiiiiild," he groaned in a voice the thief refused to recognize. The sands seemed to swell about his ankles with each utterance from his cadaverous companion. "How... came youuuuu... to the fields of the dead...?"

For all the whirlwinds' might, at once, all but the spectre seemed to have gone suddenly silent. The thief could have heard a bird take flight a mile away. Yet the winds themselves intensified.

Xerdes swallowed a mouthful of sand and repossessed himself about as well as one in the throes of utter terror can.

"Unless the lines on my face are for show," he rejoined, fooling no one, "I'm some distance from childhood."

"Youuuu're some distance from the graaaaave."

Xerdes looked the other up and down, suppressing a retch.

"That puts me in a class of one."

The black sockets seemed to peer at him deeper than any eyes ever had. They probed past him. *Through* him. To the cowering infant beneath. The sobbing orphan Wulf had recruited as a youth, trained as a young man... and abandoned in death.

"You jest..." began the phantasm, "...to stifle your screams."

Now it was Xerdes's turn to look past his companion. Into oblivion. The one at his back and the one that awaited him.

"You will warm heart and hearth in the frozen South," Wulf cryptically prophesied. "You will converse with the damned, flee from the Serpent. Find the one with no face..."

Xerdes shook his head in bemusement.

"Getting my itinerary from beyond the grave," he chuckled, "It's fallen to this."

"You do yourself disservice to dismiss it," rejoined the spirit, "Fate is a coin with two faces. Which end faces the sun... is yours to choose."

The bony, pointing hand withdrew in silence.

"For all your fallibilities..." said the ghost, "Myyyyyyyy demise... was not your doing."

Xerdes turned his face from Wulf. He was finding it difficult to converse with death.

"Yours isn't the one I…" the thief's voice trailed off.

For a long, pregnant moment, the phantom said nothing.

When it at last spoke, its words were less spoken than hurled.

"Neither… was hers."

Xerdes spun to face the formless phantom but found he was once again alone, desolate in the eye of the whirlwind. Even in the living furnace around him, the cold caress of death permeated him to the bone.

And then he felt it. Frigid fingers clasped upon his shoulder. He spun a second time.

And found his eyes locked with a pair of piercing azure eyes. Accented by a single splash of cobalt warpaint. In quietus as in her mortal existence, she remained a portrait of Horrand beauty. Her shredded cloak hung in tatters about her broken body. Blood-matted ringlets of sallow blonde tumbled down her lifeless visage. Her wintry pallor in life had taken on the waxen glow of the grave.

Saryss.

The ground gave a lurch, and Xerdes was alarmed to find it swollen about his ankles and was closing steadily.

"Do not look down," Saryss half-whispered, half-sang, "but turn your eyes upward. *Ascend*."

Long, sickly digits took hold of the clasp of the tattered cloak wound about her uneven shoulders. As she undid it, and the cape billowed into the wind, Xerdes shuddered at the mangled state of her gnarled corpse.

The thing that had been Saryss pressed the metal clasp into the palm of her lover's right hand.

"Bear it…" she whispered melodically, as if in concert with the wind, "…in lieu of your guilt."

Icy digits took hold of his hand and gently folded them around the metal trinket. Of Horrand make, it was so massive that it covered nearly the circumference of his entire hand. The parted lovers were suddenly buffeted by a massive gust, rendering all about them invisible.

He felt a chest without a heartbeat pressed to his breast.

A mouth without warmth pushed against his.

A single, frigid kiss.

Xerdes was tempted to let it linger, but the crawling sensation deep in his throat told him to pull away. Suddenly, his cheeks bulged with a putrid, writhing mass, and he felt a bitter acidity stinging the back of his throat. He spat reflexively. Before his widening eyes, the vomitous sputum began to reel and skitter upon the ground.

Maggots.

"My... lov...."

The winds were unceasing now, deafening them both in a sea of sodden dust. The wavering form of Saryss slowly vanished before his welling eyes.

Xerdes could only watch her go.

The whispers on the wind intensified in number and volume while ancient tongues and arcane incantations from long-dead throats ululated about his brain. He saw twisted forms among the sodden nothingness, shadow-forms of the long-dead legions of the Valen Empire, abandoned by their king to perish in this forsaken soil, their mouths agape as if still reeling from the betrayal after all these years. Then a solitary voice rose about the din. A whisper-scream erupting from a vengeful, sand-split throat.

"XEEEERDEEEEEESSSSSSSSS..."

Exploding through the spectral sandstorm sprang a figure shrouded entirely in gray. At his haggard side, dangling limply, was a silver blade. Xerdes's dumbstruck thoughts raced in a vain attempt to place the familiar sight.

The Wraith did not afford him time to speculate.

An unyielding blow struck at his side, catching him entirely unawares. Had the blade not caught a glint of wavering sunlight, he may not have moved in time to avoid it. Instead, the thief staggered to the side, awkwardly circumnavigating the sands that still seemed to reel about their newly joined combat. Off-balance, Xerdes cartwheeled head over heel to the ground in a cacophony of powdery dust.

The Ghostwind belted them both, all but pinning Xerdes to the spot upon which he landed. The Wraith stood stolid at the heart of it, readying his blade in a fighting style the thief dimly recognized. Unfazed by the gale, it was as if he had been birthed by the breath of the ancient dead, long since disintegrated into the very fume they both breathed in this timeworn desert.

He heard ragged breathing from beneath the billowing cloak. Witnessed an awkward, one-sided gait encroach steadily forward. Saw the blade level in a heavily bandaged arm, expertly balanced with the

"Bear it..." she whispered melodically, as if in concert with the wind, "...in lieu of your guilt."

point held laterally forward. Shoulders straightening. Back arching upright.

The stance of a practiced swordsman.

The Wraith stabbed at his adversary's heart with a snarl, and the thief pulled his dagger free just in time to catch his bladepoint with the hilt and sent the shrouded form sprawling past. As the gray shade crossed harmlessly to his right side, it drew just near enough for Xerdes to spot a smooth, white ceramic mask beneath a fluttering hood, concealing the entirety of his face. In the violent blur, he could discern only that its surface was utterly smooth and featureless, save two thin black slits that arced laterally across for the sake of vision. As Xerdes spun back to his feet, he looked more closely at his nameless threat.

Through hails of stinging sandspray, the Wraith suddenly doubled spasmodically, leaning awkwardly to his side. Where his left arm should be. Naught hung there but the tattered edges of an ashen cloak. Burying his swordpoint in the ground to steady himself, the thief thought he saw the shifting sands swell suddenly and then recede. Whatever the Ghost Wind was, it seemed to cause the ground to come alive as well.

From beneath the mask, he heard a faint voice hiss the words, "You... are a dead man. Plundering a dead castle. Communing with corpses. In a dead country..."

"I get it. I'm dead." Xerdes rejoined.

The thief heard a single expulsion of air seethe against the inside of the ceramic mask.

Another volley of sword strikes fired from beneath the blinding cloak. Xerdes spun sideways, nowhere near as deftly as intended, managing to deflect the last of these with the unbridled kinetic force of a neutered housecat. He was fighting a losing battle. The Wraith knew it.

He felt a brutal blow to the middle of his shoulders as he spun and found himself catapulting headfirst into the turbid dunes still whirling about them. Only the last-minute stiffening of his knees preventing him from being embedded up to his neck in quicksand. The ground gave. It didn't give much. When his head emerged from the mire, his hood didn't come with it.

DEATH MASK

The Wraith

Even through fine granules of dust, Xerdes could distinguish the murderous spectre lurching unevenly toward him, blade point half-dragging along the ground to one side. Steadily, calmly, inevitably as the call of the grave. Half-blinded by the sand still caked to his sweat-soaked brow, he made to wipe his eyes... and suddenly paused. The Wraith had pulled close enough to blot out what little orange light remained of an utterly obscured sun. Beneath the hood, the featureless mask seemed to consider the sight. The thief had paused perfectly in place. His right arm was held to his brow, and his head had lowered defeatedly while his left propped him up right.

Or so the spectre thought.

THE GHOSTWIND

Suddenly, Xerdes's gloved hand dug deep into the dunes he sat all but swallowed by and emerged with a fistful of fine soil. The cloud of concentrated dust shot like a trebuchet missile from his fist. Directly into the concealed features of the faceless assailant. The Wraith recoiled with a hellish shriek, nearly doubling backward as aculeate particles of silt stung at his eyes through the narrow apertures that, until now, had facilitated his vision, throwing off his hood as he did so.

Amidst the stinging sandspray, Xerdes could make out little of his exposed head, save long and matted strands of hair, pulled back and away from the masked face by a length of what looked like leather cord. One entire side of the skull seemed bare, either shorn by a knife of some other wound. Slowly, a dawning of realization awakened in Xerdes's mind. The irregular movements, the shuffling gait. This creature was most certainly a man. But one who had been injured beyond most human endurance. As wrapped fingers frantically cleared the gravelly fume from his mask, the Wraith suddenly reached deep within the folds of his cloak and within moments, produced an object it took a moment for Xerdes to fully recognize: a fluidly curving dagger of Nazgan make. Spots of dried blood still clung stubbornly to its tip, now commingling with rust.

Xerdes's eyes narrowed in bewilderment as he slowly tried to piece together the madman's identity. And how he would have come by his former weapon.

Recognizing his opponent was off guard, the Wraith abruptly hurled the dagger directly at the thief's heart. A split-second decision to leap to his feet was the only thing that saved Xerdes from certain death. The dagger point bored deep into the dune he had been perched upon and stayed there. Xerdes sprang so errantly in his exhaustion that he misjudged the precipice and tumbled backward, crumpling upon the back of his neck and already slipping from consciousness. Just before the end, through clouded eyes, he witnessed a strange sight.

The dune moved. Confused, the Wraith's maddened eyes narrowed in dismay as all about him, the hills of the A'lidar seemed to encircle his kneeling frame.

Then with a violent explosion, the claws of the desert were all about him. Coiled about his legs, crushing his side, pulling him inexorably into the womb of the earth. The ground had not been shifting under the force of the Ghostwind at all… but a mere topsoil, concealing a mammoth, slumbering Windserpent of Nazgan.

The Wraith that was once a man dissolved into the ether, still crumpling in the sinuous coils of the ravenous beast. His hips were swallowed whole. His chest constrained beneath the sodden mire. In a single, vicious wrenching motion, his masked face and reddened eyes receded beneath the sea of glass. The final victim of his own mysterious, misguided revenge.

As nameless in life as he was in death.

With a futile effort to raise his limp neck, the thief's head again sank to the ground.

Then his eyes shuttered to perfect blackness, and Xerdes knew no more.

Chapter 7
Monsoon of the Mind

Maeday, 4th of Torgan
1856

A feeling of fingers fumbling at the thief's belt were the first indication Xerdes was not yet dead.

Smooth, scaly fingers. Fingers that weren't his.

Even in his bleary-eyed, windblown state, Xerdes wheeled and drew his dagger in one fluid motion. Or rather would have had his dagger remained in a sheathe at his side.

His was evidently a circumspect assailant.

"You will find no weapon, wayfarer," he heard the man hiss from beneath a sackcloth hood, needing no visual confirmation to discern he was a Bord.

"Let me guess," Xerdes said, sizing up his recent run of luck. "You're also with the Afa?"

A giddy, lilting laugh erupted from the lungs of the sun-maddened man. As he threw his head back, the hood fell with it, and a bald, reptilian skull glimmered beneath. Pale amber eyes narrowed incredulously at his ostensible captive.

"By the Salar, no!" he said, "I am but a traveling... merchant. An economic nomad, you see."

"What do you trade in? Muggings?"

"Anything I find lying around" said the Bord, with a serpentine leer.

Xerdes could see he was going to like this one.

Shielding his brow with his forearm, the thief could now see the whispering winds were gone. There was an utter, immobile stillness to the air he'd not beheld since first arriving at the forsaken estate to begin with. The dust devil had cleared; the ghostwinds had ceased. In their place, the sun leered down like bloodshot eyes, wavering in the early evening light, almost near enough to headbutt.

A line of dainty footprints at his back answered the other question already taking shape in Xerdes's muddled mind. Some 10 feet distant, manacled at the wrist and ankles, Sháiná struggled at the end of a rope. A rope which the Bord "merchant" firmly clasped in his reptilian toils. Her crimson mouth had been mercifully stifled by a knotted rag which was impressively putrid. Her already revealing regalia seemed somehow even more lurid than before. The low-cut blouse had shredded at both sides, all but baring her breasts, and what had been the skirt end of a flowing scarlet gown was torn at either end, leaving little but a lengthy loincloth to preserve her feminine humility. Or whatever qualified as humility to Sháiná.

"And where are you off with her? A convent?"

Rows of jagged teeth spread into a razor-sharp grin.

"The K'ras Council[1] willing, the Kara'Zin Court."

"...and I'd wager not as a dignitary," Xerdes enjoined.

"Let's just say there's... been no abundance of pleasure women at court since a female was crowned as Sálár."

"She's brought me many things, pal," Xerdes cautioned mockingly, "Pleasure isn't one of them."

Even with her mouth gagged, Sháiná emitted a hiss worthy of a windserpent. Xerdes admired the effort momentarily, then continued, "...and are all the Salar's subjects referring to the sovereign ruler of Nazgan as if she were anything other than divine, these days? I thought that was grounds for–"

"I know well what it is, waylander. Yet who will execute sentence this far from the throne?" the Bord fired back. "The sands?"

Xerdes smirked and answered with a violent kick to his abductor's knees. Bords being built vastly stronger in the upper body and only tangentially supported by comparatively weak hindquarters, much like a great ape, the target of his assault was well selected. He heard the Bord's brittle shin bones pop backward. A high-pitched shriek tore from his reptilian throat as he collapsed and caught a mouthful of dune, cartwheeling in abject agony.

---

[1] **The K'ras Council:** A 12-person committee of landed Nazgan nobles, second in authority only to the Sálár herself.

The thief wasted no time, mounting his Bord assailant and pinning him to the earth with an elbow to the throat. A weak, sputtering hiss lolled from his lips as reptilian slits spat silent venom at him.

"So," said the thief, the fog in his head gradually beginning to clear, "We'll want to talk."

A faint gurgling sound was the Bord's only retort.

Xerdes lifted his arm from his collarbone slightly and allowed him a second attempt.

"W… why… why would y…?" he groused impotently, "…I did not intend to *kill* you."

"Just audition me for the role of royal chamberboy," speculated Xerdes.

The vacant glare from the Bord beneath him told the thief he'd hit near the mark.

"J… just let me… go…" the merchant groveled, "I was already evacuating when I saw you bo—"

"Evacuating from what? A light breeze?"

The Bord briefly stopped struggling with his long, lithe forearms and indicated to Xerdes's immediate left. He seemed to be referencing the Citadel, still half-submerged in a pool of still water.

"C… can you not see?" he squealed desperately. "The Shinni. What the smoothfaces call an earthquake! 'The Cataclysm', as the priests say! The f-flood… f-from underground caverns… deep beneath the Hela mines, hundreds of miles below the s-surface! After the tremors, it seeps in and d… drowns… what little farmland can be cultivated here! Then… then the serpents came."

He awkwardly adjusted the arm on his throat, struggling for breath, before concluding, "I am a merchant, waylander. I make my living selling to the farmers. And I am no match for the windserpents! I… I had no choice but to go!"

Many things dawned on Xerdes at once. None of them pleasant.

"I… was contracted to come here," he muttered, half to himself.

"And did you not ask why it would be dangerous enough that they needed to p… pay?"

With his left hand, the thief reached into a sash at the merchant's belt, and removed his stolen dagger, still in its scabbard. Then he slowly removed his forearm from the Bord's throat.

DEATH MASK

"You are not the first to be sent to the Nat'In," added the merchant, caressing his bruised neck, "Legends persist about the contents of its vault."

"…and, for once, they're not exaggerated."

"So too are tales told of its legendary dangers," the Bord said. It hadn't taken long for a crafty smile to work its way back across his face.

"Neither are they," Xerdes replied, shaking his head at his own naivete.

"Had you not wondered why a mansion would lie so distant from the capitol?" crooned the Bord. "Why the Salar would even *want* to seize it? And why only the windserpents could frighten them away?"

"When government is involved, what's wrong with simple robbery for a motive?"

"Oh, but it is. But not of some sagging mansion embedded in the dunes of A'lidar. But the Hela mines. The ore can be distilled into Ja'naraz[2], whose secrets only our finest smiths have yet unlocked. But…"

Xerdes's muddled brain labored to keep up. The Bord grinned wide. He did not wait.

"…it is doubly useful as a Zhi'ha[3]. During the Cataclysm, this entire country was swallowed by the under-ocean deep beneath our feet. Waves that spanned the sky crashed deep into the A'lidar. It is said that is where the serpents sprang from. To you, it is but a pool. But when the earth shook, the waters mingled with the mines. Priceless Hela essence is steeped into every ounce of ground water in this country. One drink… and you will lose yourself to the visions… or madness…"

"But I… haven't had water in hours," Xerdes rasped.

"The Hela nectar. A unique bargain among narcotics," grinned the Bord. "Even after its effects have dissipated… you may find its visions suddenly haunt or delight you all over again. Days. Even *years* later."

---

[2] **Ja'naraz:** A special manner of spring steel forged of Hela ore. Extremely pliable and resistant to decay, its mysteries have been jealously guarded by 10 centuries of Bord blacksmiths.

[3] **Zhi'ha:** The Bord word for narcotic. There is a vibrant trade of it, particularly in Nazgan, where it was once a legitimate and accepted practice dispensed legally by priests.

58

Xerdes stared in disbelief into the distance. The phantasms. The eerie lights of the vault. The strange shapes dancing at the corners of his vision. The spectres of Wulf and Saryss.

It had all been some waking fever-dream induced by drugs in the waters of the courtyard.

Certain he'd regained his grip on reality, Xerdes's eyes trained on his adversary.

Bords weren't the only thieves in the deserts of A'lidar, and compared to Xerdes, they were rank amateurs. Intending to turn the tables on the Bord, he reached with his right hand to draw his recovered dagger from his belt.

Something tumbled from his hand and struck the sand as he did.

Xerdes looked down, completely unaware he had been holding it the entire time.

The intricate knotwork of a Horrand steel clasp, one meant for a woman's cloak, caught the sun. He dared not say, even to himself, who it had belonged to in life.

For a single, breathless moment, he stared at it intently, as if the inanimate object would somehow attack him unawares.

Then he withdrew his hand from his belt, bent over, and picked up the big trinket without allowing himself to look at it once. Xerdes turned from his former captor, gripped the rope that held the bound and gagged Sháiná, and began to walk.

He turned in a direction he was implicitly certain led back to the treacherous Kara'Zin. And the innkeeper who had employed him for a simple errand... and nearly cost him his mind and his life.

Then, a shivering Sháiná at his side, the thief walked silently amid the dunes, ambling with steadily regaining surety out into the dawning twilight.

The Whispering Waste beckoned in becalmed, stoic menace.

Xerdes walked directly into it without a word.

Chapter 8
Ambush at Xirfán

Ashday, 5th of Torgan
1856

For hours they trekked, aware the water collected from the Dead Citadel was contaminated by Hela ore and thus undrinkable. Speed being their only salvation, the two were hopeful they would survive the days' march to Kara'Zin if they simply paced themselves and conserved their remaining strength.

By the end of the following day, they knew they would be fortunate to survive the attempt.

Then, amid the sun-baked badlands, a single, wavering image met their eyes. More mirage than reality, at first they refused to believe it was actual.

Yet as they soldiered forward, mouths dried and skin stinging from the day's march in the midday sun, it failed to disappear. And then they saw them.

The towering trunks of Lonná trees, their angular fronds flapping in the harsh desert wind.

A tropical tree, to be sure. But one incapable of growing far away from water.

They quickened their pace to the point of stumbling, and more than once, Xerdes had to stoop and grab Sháiná by the arm to avoid abandoning her in the deathly expanse of the A'lidar Desert.

Then the welcome glare of afternoon sun reflected from the waters of a large pond bid them welcome.

They had reached the Xirfán oasis, the midpoint between Kara'Zin and Tralini and the restpoint for many a bedraggled pilgrim traversing the desolate country of Nagzan.

His knees hit the water's edge like a sledgehammer.

"Don't gorge yourself," he warned, already dipping to drink.

DEATH MASK

Sháiná's thirst was already halfway to sated by the time he offered the unbidden advice.

From driftwood and a cloak he kept packed away in his knapsack, Xerdes fashioned a lean-to, whereupon the thief and his recovered quarry all but collapsed in dehydrated exhaustion. At their stilted pace, neither could have guessed how distant the city remained. Low in the valley of Chathra, it was all but invisible on the horizon, even if someone were 20 miles outside the city walls. Only the great spire of the Zi'Zin clambering to the heavens would betray its presence as travelers neared the final miles of their journey.

Xerdes and Sháiná had spied naught but blinding sand for hours, and the verdant oasis told them they would near their destination in several more.

Finally looking up from his labors, Xerdes could see a smattering of other travelers all about the water's edge, along with a mottled conglomeration of fauna dipping to drink in the forbidding environment.

They hailed from all lands and bore all manner of dress, but Bords and swarthy men of the high country of Nazgan's North prevailed. The nomads of the north made frequent traffic with Kara'Zin, and the hospitable waters of Xirfán made their repeated trips possible. Among them, a line of slaves—latched at the neck to a pair of wooden boards borne about their shoulders—waited patiently for their turn at the watering hole before doubtless being shuttled off to die in the Sálár's silver mines. The slaves were likewise from all lands. there were several humans and more than a few Bords. there was even a single half-starved Ferás-sûn[1]. An open practice across Nazgan, the sight of slavery nevertheless made the thief's lip curl in instinctive revulsion.

Xerdes leaned back and let out a sigh that carried with it every burden of the preceding week. He had not reclined for a full minute before he felt a soft, feminine form nestling at his side.

---

[1] **Ferás-sûn:** The wolven, clannish folk who predominately dwell in the northern country of Highcrest. The size of a human, they are otherwise wolflike in appearance. A fractured, honorific culture, they were once the slaves of the Aviári, even speaking a variant of their language, but they ultimately rebelled, splitting into distinctive clans with their own dialects, civic structures, and religions.

No sooner had he parted his leaden eyelids than Sháiná's charcoal eyes intercepted their gaze. Wide and expectant, hers were the kind of eyes that didn't ask. They demanded.

"You have decided then," she said in an accent like velvet cyanide.

"What? The wine I want to pair with your noose?"

Her brow furrowed, "Pardon...?"

"The one you've been figuring out how to fit around my neck since we left the estate, I mean."

It took her a moment to process the insult. She shot him a look he felt between his shoulder blades.

"You are a tiresome cur," she ejaculated.

"Yeah, my priest is always telling me that."

She looked back out across the oasis at a group of Bords fastening saddles to their horses at the water's edge, as if momentarily lost in a reverie.

"He's not the man you think he is, you know."

"I'll pretend to know who you mean," Xerdes replied, his eyes already closing again.

"Azin," she specified, "Not a man of ambition. Or looks. Or means. But it's worse than all that. His every action is counterfeit."

"What, like that bit of colored glass on his finger he's passing off as a noble's ring?"

She started, apparently impressed by his observational skills.

"Most are taken in by that 'deposed L'Intáza noble' routine," she said. "Why did you agree to come after me if you didn't?"

"Maybe I hoped to find something worth missing," he sighed, folding his hands behind his head. "... or someone."

She didn't miss the bait and curled her body even closer.

"And... have you?"

He cocked a half-open eye in her direction and replied, "Suppose I'm just waiting for all the cards to be out on the table before I wager."

"I suppose you still don't trust me," she swooned with the authenticity of wax fruit.

"We'll leave that an open question."

"What if I told you," she began with a heavy pause, "...that it is *I* who am, in fact, the noble? That Azin married me to ingratiate himself with the council? That all my... *escapades*... have happened with his full knowledge, if not necessarily consent?"

DEATH MASK

He closed his eyes and permitted himself a muted grin.

"All my affairs. All my... adventures... and yet I desire only my *freedom*. To be away from him. To no longer labor as any man's vessel, plaything, or weapon in some... political game..." she said in a hushed whisper, and Xerdes felt a wet pool soaking into the shoulder of his jerkin.

It seemed right. Which was half the problem.

It had the hollow, fastidious order only a lie can boast. It lacked the slovenly briar of fact.

He opened his eyes and really took her in. Even with shredded sleeves and tattered sandals, she was a dusky raven-haired vision. Amid the human flotsam about the oasis, wreathed by the windswept dunes of A'lidar, she fit in like a wedding gown at an orgy.

"You agreed to the marriage... then act as if it's a trap?"

She shrugged hopelessly and looked at the ceiling of the half-tent contemplatively.

"Name a snare more dangerous than the one you spring on yourself."

"And... Kevelin?" Xerdes pried, "I can think of softer shoulders to cry on if it's liberation you're after."

Sháiná scoffed sardonically.

"Over a loveless faux-noble, wielding me like a gamepiece from a shit-caked inn? Even *you* would be an improvement," she said, leaving Xerdes to debate whether her tone was seductive or condescending. "At least *you* saved my life."

Xerdes decided to let her make what she wanted out of a wry grin.

"I suppose you could do worse," Xerdes mused.

"Don't I always?" she sighed, and he found her head now cradled against his neck, her firm breasts all but smothering his shoulder.

"What if..." she started, as if awash in doubt, "if I were to marry a man who would leave me alone *entirely*... I would finally be free to run my life. To manage my own home. To no longer be a receptacle of other men's motives."

"No, not of their *motives*..." mocked Xerdes.

"I mean it. A ceremonial marriage. To annul the farce I'm in at present... and prevent any others. With a man who wants nothing to do with me... *or* my inheritance?"

"As for instance...?"

"You," she purred. And her eyes seemed to settle on his chest and narrow in satisfaction.

"Hmmm," Xerdes let out, unsure what even he meant by it.

"You think I'm trying to make you a puppet."

"I think you're trying to make me the entire puppet show," he retorted, his fingers fumbling absently with the Horrand clasp. A gift from a phantom.

"I have seen you. Each time we have stopped. When you think I'm not looking. Toying with that trinket. Gazing at it. Whatever you're doing."

"Everyone needs a hobby."

"Who did it belong to?"

"No one you would have wanted to know."

Her hands explored down the length of his leg. She wore *pieces* of a form-fitting purple gown, and pushed her full bosom at him with the subtlety and deliberation of a herd of wild mustangs. He never looked down at her once.

It took her entirely too long to realize that her body was not irresistible, but she got there eventually. He heard an exasperated sigh escape her lips.

"You talk smart, but... you act stupid." she said with a scoff.

"...and you haven't even seen me drunk."

In petulance and frustration, she rained a single, violent blow against his chest. One that hit harder than he cared to admit.

"What happened to 'hope you can trust me'?" he exclaimed after catching his breath.

She seemed like she wanted to shout. But, stillborn, it became a heavy sob. The mask of icy seduction slid away before Xerdes's eyes and revealed the broken woman beneath. She'd played her only hand.

She'd lost.

Xerdes felt his arms wrap around her doubled body. Heard himself whisper soft reassurances. The fallen noblewoman had shattered all about him. It was all he could do to pick up the pieces.

"I..." she sputtered, "I... *hated* Kevelin."

"We ought to form a club," he commiserated.

"I... I had him take me there. Because..."

Her voice trembled and trailed off. When she continued, it was disquieted, but resolute.

"The Nat'In. The Dead Citadel. It never belonged to Azin," she said, regaining her breath between sobs, "...it belonged to me."

The final piece fell into place.

"So you returned to... take back what? Your dowry?"

"No."

"Your inheritance?"

"In a manner of speaking," she replied. "You carry it on you even now, Xerdes."

The thief knew without asking. His hands reached to the pouch at his belt. He found his fingers caressing the wealth within.

His thoughts turned once again to the coin.

The one she'd since told him was called "the Salar Silverhawk."

"Azin was desperate for it. He even hired Kevelin..."

"...and you went ahead and hired him right back. Then the two of you escaped together. Rutting like rabbits all the while... we'll say it was to secure his loyalty. All over some coin?"

"You can have it," she whispered, still choking back sobs, "It has brought more misery than riches. I only... ask you to consider... you needn't be my true husband. Only on paper. Only in a contract. You can go. Live your life. And I... I can finally begin to live *mine*."

Xerdes's mind reeled. To his dismay and alarm, he found he was actually beginning to see the logic in it. He still wasn't sold.

"...and why this coin specifically? And what makes me the lucky winner," he inquired, "when you could pick any pauper off the street and strike the selfsame arrangement? Hell, most men in Kara'Zin would marry you in the old-fashioned sense. The kind that comes with an actual *marriage*. Most men would *want* you."

"...because you're the only one who *doesn't*," she said and swallowed deeply. "How is it the only honest man I've met in months is a thief?"

"As honest as anyone can be in a world where it's a death sentence."

"Whatever you decide, whether it's apart... or with me and my many... *talents*..." she pressed on, her fingers now dancing along the edge of his neck, "Azin... he *has* to pay..."

"We'll see," he heard himself say. He knew it was a lie. He also knew she likely believed it. He'd yet to encounter a liar yet who hadn't believed every work of fiction they'd been told. Once someone divorced themselves from the truth, they never made its acquaintance again.

She muttered something else then, but Xerdes only faintly perceived it. For other voices had overtaken hers. What had been whispers outside the tent had since risen to audible voices.

The kind that were clearly conspiring.

Even in the harsh, recondite tongue of I'zakas—the most closely guarded of the Bords' many secrets—their intent was more than discernible.

"If it won't be you…" he thought he heard her purr, disregarding the sound completely.

The wall of the lean-to swept aside in a single, abrupt motion.

Standing behind them, ranks bristling with weapons, were the Bord slavers he'd spied earlier.

Xerdes wasted no time ascertaining their motivations. It was clear they were meant to join the chain gang.

His dagger came free in a flash.

The enemy's sword was quicker. A Bord blade struck his shoulder, sending a stream of blood spattering across the dirt immediately, the momentum of the stroke spinning the thief's body in the opposite direction. He managed to steady himself on a nearby tree, but it had nearly been the end of him.

Sparing no time to nurse the pain, Xerdes slashed mercilessly at the trunk of a slaver's right leg, tendons visibly severing in a fine mist of black blood. He could scarcely hear the scream of his enemy before another was upon him with the stroke of an axe.

After a timely dodge, it missed him by a hair's breadth.

A half-dozen slavers were circling the thief already, and Xerdes comprehended immediately that this was an unwinnable melee. He had but one chance to even the dismal odds.

Whirling out of the way of an oncoming sword, Xerdes positioned himself directly behind the slave line. In a single, arcing stroke, he severed the cord that bound the chain gang together.

Slaves, both Bord and Man, young and infirm, wasted no time in waylaying their captors.

The fracas erupted immediately. Out of the corner of his eyes, Xerdes saw Sháiná wisely scurrying behind a tree at the water's edge. The slavers were so distracted by their combat that they failed to follow her.

It was quickly evident, however, that slaves make poor warriors.

" 'This is not good,' Xerdes heard himself mutter. The Ferás-sûn nodded in perfect silence."

One by one, human and Bord alike were hewn by the blades of their oppressors. To his immediate left, a boy no older than 20 was savagely decapitated when he attempted to charge a soldier while armed only with a rock. Sidestepping his head, Xerdes rejoined the battle. Parrying blade fore and aft, he stabbed one Bord in the throat, ending his life instantly, while kicking another back into the oasis, where he barely floundered afloat in his heavy chainmail.

Soon, just two lone fighters remained.

Xerdes, left arm hanging limp at his side.

And the Ferás-sûn, who had yet to utter a single word since attaining his newfound freedom. His long, scarred snout remained closed. While pale, steel-gray eyes peered knowingly at the surrounding enemies.

Shirtless and in rags, already his brown-gray fur was matted with blood, most of which belonged to his Bord slavemasters. He wielded only a single wooden walking staff purloined from a fallen enemy. Though weakened, he was awash in placid calm. Controlled. Expert. Starvation had stolen his strength but not his technique. His were the movements of a master practitioner of the Ferás-sûn martial arts.

However he'd come to his present predicament, he had clearly not gone willingly.

A Bord with a sloped helm atop his brow began to direct the attack. Every opening unwittingly offered by Xerdes and his newly freed companion was suddenly exploited. Every strike was followed up with a reprisal. Soon, the thief sagged to the earth, utterly overcome by the overpowering attack. The Ferás-sûn—still mute amid the onslaught— soon joined him. Blood streamed from multiple sword wounds in their chest, shoulders, and thighs. The dagger threatened to tumble from Xerdes's quavering fingers.

Then the man in the helm held up a single fist.

The assault stopped.

Through his own ragged gasps, Xerdes heard a commotion at the edge of the din. Even the helm-bedecked man he now took to be a captain looked off to the side.

To the treeline.

To Sháiná.

"D... don't..." the thief panted, his mouth unable to form a coherent warning.

AMBUSH AT XIRFÁN

To his horror, he watched the bronze-skinned beauty emerge from behind the tree. Hands in the air. From this remove, he at last saw the full measure of the state she was in. Diaphanous rags fluttered about her curvaceous frame. Her skin bronzed by the sun rendered her even darker than usual. Yet somehow not a hair on her head was out of place.

He heard the captain shout something in I'zakas.

Shout something and then indicate toward the two half-dead fighters.

Sháiná slinked slowly, deliberately toward the man in evident surrender.

Then, with a single word, her hands fell.

The captain gave her a single bow.

A *low* bow.

"This is not good," Xerdes heard himself mutter.

The Ferás-sùn nodded in perfect silence.

The next words Sháiná spoke were low. Steady.

She spoke in the language of the Bords.

"You're right about one thing," Xerdes coughed. "You *are* a woman of many talents."

"It's a shame I never showed you half of them."

"When did you learn to speak *Slaver*?"

She permitted herself a tasteful chuckle before answering,

"My sweet, handsome thief."

He didn't like anything she said that came with a compliment.

"I don't speak Slaver." A playful smirk pulled at her pouting lips, "I speak *Afa*."

The thief fell deathly silent. Only now did he comprehend the depths of his predicament. The Afa—the most powerful criminal cartel in Nazgan, one of the four branches of the Salar's government, whose sole dominion it was to regulate and tax all thievery in Nazgan, making Xerdes a living affront—had pursued him across the A'lidar dunes but had lost him among the Ghostwinds. And now Sháiná had marched him right back into their waiting arms.

Xerdes felt a fistful of his hair being yanked by an unknown assailant at his back. he felt himself being pulled from his knees by the Bord assassins.

Xerdes spat blood through split lips and chuckled darkly.

71

"…afraid I'm going to have to reject the wedding proposal."
The siren simply folded her arms.
"I'm so sorry for all that is about to happen."

Chapter 9
Rattle of Chains

Trisday, 8th of Torgan
1856

The days that followed were a beclouded nightmare. Just as well, as they were not the kind Xerdes wished to commit to memory. For three days and nights, all he knew was cold steel manacles suspending his languid body from the dungeon ceiling and the sickening crack as his shoulders and elbows slipped periodically from their sockets each time he was struck. Which he found was not an infrequent experience.

His captor knew exactly how to do it.

The Afa had spared no expense in his interrogation. They could afford it. For half a week, he'd been treated to the peerless hospitality of the Black Hood of Nazgan.

Inquisitor.

Interrogator.

Torturer.

With the fashion sense to match.

He was a lumbering hulk of a man. Sinews bulged beneath taut skin. He was so large that Xerdes was tempted to assume his Horrand ancestry but for his jet-black complexion. One impossible to ascertain from a face that remained perpetually shrouded by a black executioner's hood. In the long years of the Afa's dominion in Nazgan, he had gone from dutiful footsoldier to elite enforcer... and finally to living legend.

The bloody kind.

The purpose of his inquisition was apparent before his feet touched the dust-strewn streets of Kara'Zin once again. They wanted something.

An object.

A coin of aurous silver. Emblazoned with a single hawk.

Scarcely a crevice of his body had remained unchecked. His belongings had long since been disposed of. Yet still they had failed to find the object of their search.

Which was just as well, reasoned Xerdes, considering it was the only reason he still lived. The thief wasn't alone. Chained to the wall opposite, positioned more comfortably than his current position, strung up like a human piece of poultry... was the passive face of the half-starved Ferás-sûn. His wolven prison companion had put on a few pounds even in the few days since their imprisonment, meals being brought more regularly than on a chain gang. Yet he was still dangerously lean, and the sackcloth pantaloons roped about his legs still hung visibly from his famished frame. One of his high, canine ears had been split by a sword some years previous and long since scarred over, but his otherwise unblemished face, replete with pale gray eyes and a long, firm snout, betrayed no emotion whatso-ever. The most he found he could elicit was a single nod or shake of the wolf-man's head.

It was now clear the man was a mute. That was just as well since most Ferás-sûn spoke their uniquely accented woodland variant of the Aviári[1] tongue to begin with. In any event, the thief found a lopsided conversa-tion preferable to none. His partner probably would have disagreed.

Xerdes had even given him a name.

Tián.

One of the few Aven words Xerdes had picked up in his travels and a rough approximation of the term "friend." Given the Bords' policy toward their servants, it was entirely possible this was the first name he had ever been given. To say Tián was emotionless was, in fact, a redundancy. Even waylanders and those who had never crossed the Valen border were familiar with rumors of the forest dwellers' peculiar meditation practices. The sáidán, they reputedly called it. How they permitted themselves not a single emotion through the course of the average day, preferring cold reason to reflexive, emotionally informed action. Then, usually before lying down to rest... expelled whatever cataclysmic eruption of rage, happiness, love, or anguish they had accu-mulated over the course of the preceding day.

---

[1] **Aviári:** The flighted folk of northern Highcrest. Fair, austere, and one of the few races of Trávinás who still assert the efficacy of the arcane arts. Once the mightiest empire on the continent, centuries of war with the Horrands, humans, and their for-mer slaves, the Ferás-sûn, have left them cloistered and isolationist in their mountain strongholds.

Tián

Xerdes was halfway to suspecting it was a myth, having not witnessed Tián performing the feat even once since their arrival. Though he had often caught his fellow captive with closed eyes, sitting utterly erect, as if peering out into nothingness.

The massive, blackened iron door at the far corner of the room suddenly jolted, groaning outward on its huge hinges. Torchlight spilled into the dimly illuminated expanse. It was fleeting.

For the colossal silhouette of the Black Hood soon filled the barrier. In both meaty paws, a weighty claymore was clasped. He assumed it wasn't a gift.

The walking mass wasn't alone. Behind him, and back a distance, loomed a lithe and spindly figure draped in flowing robes. As the two traversed the room, he saw that the mauger man was bearded, about his age, with the bronzed complexion typical of the men of this region.

75

About his neck, wrists, and all ten fingers glimmered just enough gold jewelry to make a man drown on an evening swim but not quite enough to open a store.

His long, flowing tresses were the color of onyx and pulled back high from an impressive piece of forehead. High, sallow cheekbones were headed in the same direction.

"U'Bar tells me you have been less than forthcoming," the new arrival's buttery voice soothed.

"I'll pretend to know who that is," said the thief with a leer.

"The man that once was," enjoined his apparent jailer, "who now shields the world, as much as himself, beneath the Black Hood."

"All lies," chuckled Xerdes, "I'm awash with cooperation wherever a torturer's involved."

"Yet still you withhold the Hawk of L'Intaza," the robed man hissed, his velvety voice taking on a harsher texture, "To what end, I wonder?"

"To the end that I don't know where, or what, that is."

The robed man simply turned to his left and nodded to the Black Hood. In a single, robotic motion, the torturer reached up and freed the thief's right wrist from the steel restraints. There came a sickening crack as his shoulder sank back into socket, forced down to his side by the Black Hood's brutal effort. The thief bit his tongue but could not fully suppress a scream, managing to salvage as much dignity in the process as a prostitute at port. He could see out of the corner of his eye the claymore being set in a small brazier filled with coal.

As his arm settled at his side, gradually, feeling returned to formerly lifeless fingers.

"I can bring you comfort, thief. Even spare your life," he heard the man say amidst his pangs of agony, "...or..."

The Black Hood wrenched his wrist forward, onto a tall wooden table that sat roughly at chest level. Spreading the thief's hand flat with his thick, sausagelike digits, the mammoth interrogator reached backward and withdrew his claymore from the smoldering coals.

He pressed the tip softly against the exposed flesh of Xerdes's pinky finger. A light sizzling sound was heard, and a strange, acrid stench filled the air.

The glare Xerdes threw back into his captor's jet-black eyes never wavered.

"My name is O'Nan," he said, without needing to.

Only O'Nan, notorious crimelord of the Afa, would carry himself with such authority and ease amid this palace of perfidy. Even blindfolded on the initial trip, Xerdes knew precisely where he was. There were only so many places in the world that fit the description of the Dungeons of Da'Kan. An underground spire, only a few floors above the earth... but dozens beneath. Inside which a hellish honeycomb of winding corridors and staircases to nowhere sprawled to eternity. To killing rooms. To rape chambers. To body pits, slave quarters, and places where one would pine for the sweet release of death.

"Tell me," groaned Xerdes. "When did you start playing house with an innkeeper's wife?"

It was a shot in the dark.

The look in O'Nan's eyes told him it had hit the bullseye.

"You answer my offer with impudence," O'Nan exclaimed coolly, "Sháiná is happier here than she ever was in that rat's nest of an inn. And she's spent her nights here at *least* as long. The Hawk of L'Intaza is not your affair, outdweller. You are not of Nazgan. Well..."

And he caught a wry smile on the face of the crimelord as O'Nan added, "Not *anymore*."

The word L'Intaza had set the thief's mind to work. The words Azin the innkeeper had spoken. Of a long-deposed nobility. But it triggered even more in his mind. A litany of childhood memories. Bedtime tales, whose historical merit was dubious at best.

"Surely you're familiar with the Long Seasons of War, master thief?" O'Nan asked, partly to hear his own voice, "We were once a *power* in this part of the world. Nazgan may be mottled, but its silver veins are the richest by an order of magnitude."

"...and we can see how well that's working out."

"It once was!" O'Nan shouted, "That all ended when the Bords came. Installed their Sálár. By the end, it was a war against all. Its neighbors. Its colonies. And finally, itself. We Men, who had laid the first bricks in the foundation of Kara'Zin, fought to retain it!"

"And how'd that go?" Xerdes laughed, spitting a marbled mixture of saliva and blood on the stone floor.

"Generations later, we still speak of the stalemate," O'Nan continued, heedless of the thief's proddings, "My people knew well that we could

not keep it up. Not so long as Bords held our capitol and all the...
resources... therein. So... a peace offering was proffered. Something...
both ceremonial... and material. Something both sides respected and
sought. Something to symbolize our intent to unify... yet could easily be
bartered in accordance with our culture..."

"Something," interrupted the thief, his brow furrowing as it all came
together, "...like a coin."

"Calling the Silverhawk a mere 'coin' is like calling the ocean 'water',
sir," O'Nan answered, shaking his head, "It was both symbol and incentive.
The *perfect* symbol. And its... sudden theft, by one of our own... likewise
became the perfect symbol of our disunity and inevitable defeat. For
defeated we are. So..."

O'Nan leaned in close to his prisoner, the perfume of garlic all but
gagging him as he did.

"...you can understand why I would be... aggrieved... to lack your
cooperation. When its recovery is in prospect."

"What can I say?" Xerdes sighed, "I'm fresh out of Silverhawks."

The prince of crime spun on his back heel, robes flowing about him as
he did. After giving a subtle gesture to the Black Hood, he made for the
door.

"My proposition is simple, filcher," he said, steadying his hand against
the doorframe, "Every time you fail to help us recover what we have lost,
you will lose something of your own."

The edge of the blade again sizzled against Xerdes' finger.

"And like the Hawk... I promise it cannot be replaced."

The metal barrier slammed shut behind him with a flourish, and
Xerdes found himself once again face to face with his interrogator.

He could see the giant's broad chest swell with excitement, see the
cloth sucking in and out of his mouth as his breathing grew more harried
and manic. He doubted he was in for a massage.

U'Bar, the Black Hood of Nazgan, went to work.

Snatching Xerdes by the throat with a single, rippling right arm, he
depressed the edge of the claymore against his finger with the other.
Pulling the thief within a ragged breath, his ears perceived a single, low,
throaty rumble, emanating from somewhere beneath the hidden depths
of the hood.

"...Whhhhheeeeeeeeeerrrrrreeeeeeeeeeeee...?"

Three days of agony had taught the thief that his host had no habit of asking twice.

Tián suddenly sat erect against the wall to his right.

The Black Hood stood stoic. As if only the words of his prisoner could spur him to motion.

Then, with a cold exigence, he slammed the head of the claymore down, severing Xerdes' finger in one clean slice. A scream threatened to erupt from his throat, but for the hunk of flesh he tore out, biting down on the inside of his cheek. He wrenched away so violently, he felt his left shoulder slip again from its socket. The dull pop as bone detached from sinew resounded in the darksome corridors of the Dungeons of Da'Kan.

Then, through rolling pangs of throbbing pain, Xerdes noticed something.

The dislocation of his shoulder had put him closer to his captor, who bent now, above his own severed digit, admiring the surgical precision of the amateur amputation. Closer than Xerdes had ever been in 72 hours of agony.

Pressing up to the extreme tip of his bare left foot, Xerdes now had the leverage required to kick madly downward at the back of the Black Hooded head. The blow connected with a crack. Bent double as the inquisitor already was, his hooded face was flung far to his immediate left by the force of the strike.

Into the waiting embers of the coal pit below.

A crackling sputter of roasted flesh as it grafted itself to blackened sackcloth all but deafened the prone prisoners. The sound that tore from the Black Hood's throat as his melted face became one with his namesake could scarcely be described as human.

He catapulted in deepening shock to the stone floor, cinders broiling amid his bubbling hide.

His key ring tumbled with him.

Xerdes did not miss his moment, kicking the keys deftly over to Tián.

The Ferás-sûn captive perceived his plan exactly. Undoing his manacles in short order, he next traversed the room to do likewise for the thief. It was a nice bit of teamwork, for two strangers who hadn't yet shared a word.

They stepped over the body of the Black Hood, who by now had ceased to move.

As Xerdes—aided by his newfound ally—limped to the threshold of the doorframe, Tián held up a hand to stop him. Pressing the thief's limp left shoulder against the doorframe, a single glance told him to brace for crippling pain.

Even this wordless warning undersold the agony.

With a sudden upward lurch, Tián had used the unforgiving brickwork to reset Xerdes' shoulder back into its socket. After the spasms of torment subsided, Xerdes was sure to send a single nod Tián's way. It was the closest thing to a proper "thank you" he could presently muster.

The Ferás-sûn was careful to reclaim their bag of belongings from the chest near the door, where they had remained to taunt them lo these many days, before alighting the site of their days-long imprisonment. He had started up the stairs when Xerdes stopped him.

"Sorry, friend," winced the thief. "I'm sure you've got places to be and gardens to plant, but our illustrious host gave us the setup...."

Xerdes unslung his head from beneath Tián's arm and limped obstinately in the opposite direction.

"...now it's time for the punchline."

The crimelord lay adrift in the deepest sort of sleep—the kind that always seems to come to those with at least a hundred deaths on their conscience. All at once, O'Nan was jolted to coherence, a cold sweat already beginning to form about his eyes and forehead. The cause of his frantic comportment became obvious immediately. For he reached over, expecting to caress the silken physique of Sháiná beside him. An empty expanse of linen met his grasp instead.

The crimelord of the Afa shook the disparate possibilities from his mind, already feeling a light tremble set into his slender fingers.

And then he felt it.

A wet warmth, expanding steadily at his side.

Instinctively, he swept his hands about it, initially believing he had soiled his bed linen.

When he brought his hands up, all he could see in the dimly lit expanse was a small pool of black coursing between his fingers.

He had slumbered in a small river of blood.

RATTLE OF CHAINS

Lighting the lamp at his bedside came with considerable effort, for the intensifying tremble of his fingers blew it out more than once. Then, at once, it was lit.

As lambent illumination poured into the princely bedchambers, the crimeboss paused in place. Stretched before him. Still cupping the lamp he had only recently ignited.

His hand stood stationary, only now capable of momentarily stilling the spontaneous shiver that had seized them since awakening.

Minus one finger.

Chapter 10
Sanguine Reunion

Trisday, 8th of Torgan
1856

The look on Azin's face told the tale.

Xerdes no longer wondered why anything seemed to come as a surprise to the tavernkeep. That he stood there, drawing breath at all, was doubtless an unforeseen occurrence. All the conniving, all the scheming, from virtually all quarters of this sordid affair, had persuaded the thief to take nothing and no one for granted.

He found it no coincidence the only reliable sort he'd encountered in this entire affair was incapable of speech.

The doorway remained half-cracked. So bedraggled was his appearance, after the rigors of the preceding week, the innkeep's eyes had yet to project the light of recognition.

"Are you... Xerdes, by any chance?"

"No, the name's Periwinkle."

A bemused expression fell on the innkeep's ruddy features.

"I see the Ghostwinds have not dulled your wit."

"No, I dulled it all by myself."

"Come on inside, 'Periwinkle'. I've been expecting you."

The thief complied, still deciding whether he was stepping into a tavern or a snake pit.

Even largely emptied of patrons in the late afternoon hours before Kara'Zin remembered its nightly thirst for wine and depravity, the inn reeled with activity. A fog of pipesmoke spilled from a nameless nowhere, alcoholic voices reverberated from low ceilings, sufficient to take the edge off the sounds of rattling cutlery, shot glasses, and the clatter of earthenware. Above it all, hoofbeats on the sodden street outside thundered a steady fusillade, as they bore their oblivious occupants to nowhere in particular.

Before Azin had so much as turned, the man he had hired under false pretenses halted his unspoken explication.

"You lied. I lived. You're not the first. In my line, you won't be the last."

Xerdes seated himself with some effort and finished, "Pay me, and we part without incident."

Azin fidgeted busily at first. The soiled apron hadn't sprung to life and cleaned itself in the intervening week. The balding pate had yet to bloom into a full head of hair. From where Xerdes stood, the man who'd played the part of frantic husband to some acclaim had been as straight as a bull's back leg from the beginning.

To stifle the silence, the innkeep interjected, "Is this the part where you piece it all together in an orderly package, plucked from thin air, naming all accomplices and their motives, dispensing justice all the while...?"

Xerdes played along.

"Making it your cue to blanche in the face, draw down, and slice at my throat, admitting your entire evil plan until the city guard kick down the door and ventilate your generous gut for the entire city to see?"

Azin twitched at the mouth a single time.

"No," said Xerdes, "The only one entering the door at this point will be my friend here," and with that, he indicated to the entryway. Tián entered, pulling Sháina at his side. The woman had been less upset than eerily nervous the entire way over. It was obvious to the thief and his companion that she didn't consider her rescue to be a rescue. The lingering look the proprietor gave them said more than any "Keep Out" sign could.

"Am I expected to pay the Treedog[1], too?"

The slur made the thief's lip curl. He decided to let it roll off.

"I'm a thief. Cops like me about as much as a noble without a bribe. Sure, I'm living into the idea I'll never again pick a pocket with all five fingers," drolled the thief, "...but other than that, I'm smooth as lace curtains."

---

[1] **Treedog:** A racial slur for the Ferás-sûn. A reference to the massive Tiax trees of the Alcaire forest, which some tribes hollow out and excavate to fashion their traditional dwellings.

"I could not risk that you would say no..." said the innkeep, answering a question he was never asked. "...and word had reached me out of Menuvia that you have developed a weakness for the fairer sex... and... *sentiment* as you grow older."

Xerdes scoffed and ran gloved fingers over his three-day growth of beard.

"Aging that well, am I?"

"Don't flatter yourself," he heard Sháiná groan, walking to her husband's side. "Of all the parasites and brigands I've enlisted, none was a greater disappointment than you."

"Limber-legged whore!" Azin spat, a vicious backhand across her face, punctuating the words. "...so *this* is the new knight come to bear you away from the overweight innkeeper? Three nights with Kevelin wasn't enough to fill the Great Gorge of Nazgan?"

"Oh, I've done better than him," she said, rubbing her reddening cheek, "Better than any of you, and not by a little."

Xerdes could only laugh at the impotent offering.

"Quite a love affair. I see you both like a little truth with your fiction."

A gap-toothed grin festooned itself across Azin's ears.

"What better basis for a lie? So I have used her. Can it not also be true that I love her? She is brilliant. Clever. Beautiful beyond words—"

"...and exclusive as a tavern door," Xerdes interrupted.

Sidestepping the jibe, the innkeep continued, "Carnal love is a commodity like any other, master thief. I had a resource, and so I traded it for another."

From beneath his soiled smock, a pouch, pregnant with gold was produced. The clatter it made against the table had a sing-song quality Xerdes appreciated on an aesthetic level.

Yet the thief did not move.

With a sudden snap of his grubby fingers, an entire contingent of swarthy cutthroats emerged from every shadow in the room. Bord and human alike, they drew blades and encircled the duo. Tián did not flinch.

That made one of them.

The innkeep added, "...The coin, if you please."

"Don't!" shrieked Sháiná, "You know he wishes only to offer it to the Sálár! To have himself installed on the council!"

85

"Yes," proclaimed Azin unrepentantly, "...and I have paid *fairly* for it! A half-dozen other thieves and safecrackers have I hired. None of whom have yet survived..."

He paused, giving a dismissive look to his wife before adding, "...Most of whom *you* have known far better than *I*."

"It's your gold," Xerdes shrugged, removing a wooden box from a pouch hanging from his belt. "*Triple...* your gold. Now that I better understand your economic standing."

Azin hesitated.

Then he reached again inside his apron and produced two pouches, the same size as the first.

Evidently, he expected something like this. His kind usually did.

Xerdes wondered for a heartbeat how much more he could have pressed a member of the L'Intaza Council for.

"You would let him get *away* with it, Xerdes?" Sháiná exclaimed, "The men he's sent to their deaths?"

"What did you send me to the Afa dungeons for? Singing lessons?" Xerdes hurled back, his eyes staring daggers through her flushed face.

Scrambling to her knees, she scurried across the inn floor to the thief that had suddenly become her only apparent hope for revenge.

"If he has that power... his first act will be to put me in the *ground...*" she shouted, tugging insistently at his belt.

"Only if the chains don't fit," replied Xerdes, matter of factly.

She knelt there, gaping at him in disbelief. "Should he not pay for the people he has already put there?" was the only reply she could manage.

The thief didn't even look down.

But something stirred him to speech. Something dormant. Something he'd denied since the mess in Menuvia, and perhaps even earlier.

"I admit," he started, still not looking down at her, "I wouldn't mind right and good carrying the day. I've seen it so often from the other side; it'd make for a nice change. I'd love to see this slug drop 50 pounds crushing rocks with calloused fingers in the dungeons of Kara'Zin alongside seventy-odd other saps who picked the wrong pocket at an early age and spent every waking second repeating the mistake. You're not wrong. I'd enjoy it very much. But you and I have lived too long to think I'll see it in my lifetime. Not in Kara'Zin. Not in Nazgan. Or Vale. Not in any nation or city we'll ever see. Countries don't become countries that way."

The thief cast his gaze downward at last, and instantly, he knew.

Something was about to go very, very wrong.

Her eyes darkened. It was a look Xerdes had seen before.

"Now," he heard the vixen purr.

From the rear of the inn, a row of heads emerged. Shrouds hid reptilian faces; cloaks obscured scaled flesh. Their drawn blades distracted from both. Xerdes knew the Afa assassins had caught up with him. Sháiná had helped them do it. Whether she'd left a trail for them to follow or laid a contingency for her capture from the gambit's beginning, the thief had precious time to discern. Then they circled Azin's enforcers, and all at once, he understood.

They weren't here for him.

Azin's men spun to face them, just quickly enough to look threatening, but not quickly enough to actually earn it. Xerdes's hand fell to the hilt of his dagger.

When a single silhouette rose from behind the new arrivals.

One long, rangy limb nearly touched the looming ceiling to still them.

The hand was missing a finger.

O'Nan, Crimelord of the Afa, slinked from behind their ranks. The knowing smile splayed across his face couldn't have been pried off with a pair of smithing tongs.

Sháiná steadied her hands on her hips, pulled her scarlet lips into a half-smirk and gave Xerdes a look. He gave it right back. The orange lamplight cast the left side of her shapely body in bronze.

"Kill him and take it, will you?" scoffed Sháiná, as she watched her lover approach, "It's bad enough I had to bat my eyelashes at the imbecile. He's a loose end. Tie it." She had the face of a woman who had held all her secrets close and was letting them all out at once.

O'Nan brushed past her. Extending a single hand—the one still intact—to her husband, he said, "You've done well to lure him here, Azin."

Xerdes stood there and watched him say it. Sháiná watched even harder. Her mouth gaped in disbelief. The crimelord turned to Xerdes and added, "Now let us complete our transaction so that he and I may conduct one of our own."

"Y-you..." Sháiná faltered, slumping to the tavern floor.

DEATH MASK

O'Nan was unbothered, "This is no affair of yours, thief. You have done ably. But now one of us will take his rightful place on the council. And the other..." he indicated to Azin, "Will earn a fair finder's fee for his involvement."

"That is not what we discussed," Azin shot back, forgetting to pretend to be cordial. "I was to present the Silverhawk to the council while you... would take a percentage and rule happily from the shadows."

"I already rule. With or without the shadows," O'Nan shouted back, "Enough of this."

His hand made a sweeping gesture through the air. Xerdes instinctively drew his blade.

It nearly wasn't quick enough.

A crossbow bolt screamed from the darkness, and Xerdes, still groggy from blood loss and imprisonment, could scarcely have avoided it, were the killer a better marksman.

Then it all fell in at once.

Azin's men pounced upon the newly arrived assassins. Tables toppled, torches flew from braziers, and at the heart of the din, the thief and his mute companion stood shoulder to shoulder to battle the throng. Through it all, Tián was an island of calm. His motions fluid, his counter-attacks instinctual. Tián did more damage with a simple walking stick than a tavern stacked to the ceiling with assassins managed with bladed weaponry.

The Ferás-sûn dodged one Bord's curved sword, pinned it to the floor with his right boot, and brained him viciously about the side of the skull with his staff. The reptilian assailant catapulted to the floor in a drooling heap, mere inches from the barkeep's treacherous wife.

Sháiná saw her chance. She didn't miss it.

Taking firm grasp of the Bord's sword, she sprang to her feet, a cease-less stream of I'zákás curses pouring from her throat as she fell upon O'Nan, her every motion possessed by a desire for revenge. She was a woman who had suffered her last betrayal. Her purloined sword flew sideways, into the lean neck of the Afa crimelord she had shared a bed with and believed would make her queen of the Nazgan underworld, if not more. A fountain of cherry-red blood erupted as the sword separated his skull from his shoulders.

O'Nan, scheming to the last, had become the architect of his own death. His own puppet its mortal instrument.

Sháiná stood, bathing in the sanguine stream, drenching through her half-worn rags, clear to the skin. Her body heaved with madness and exhilaration.

At once, two of Azin's remaining cutthroats darted across the bar and seized Sháiná by each arm, the madwoman thrashing and biting them all the while.

Xerdes seized his chance, scooping up the coinpurse and its siblings and slamming the box on the table to avoid throwing it at either of them. He turned to leave the room, weapon still drawn. Tián followed his lead.

Before backing through the door to the streets of Kara'Zin, he stopped in place. Looking back one last time and indicating to the gold trinket on the inkeeper's swollen finger, he added, "You should consider replacing that with a *real* wedding ring. You deserve each other."

Tián's snout furrowed as he followed the thief to the tavern door.

The door which stood already ajar. Silently framing a haggard and hunched asymmetrical silhouette.

From beneath the blood-matted edges of the gray cloak, a silver blade dangled. An expertly crafted rapier. Its argent tip kissing the floor. As if he'd only stepped from the yawning, baleful maw of a Windserpent five minutes before and decided to stop in for a pint with a side of murder.

The Wraith had survived.

The obsidian scales of a windserpent hide he spied, newly bespiraled about the hilt of the apparition's argent blade told the thief precisely how.

Something heavier than dread settled in Xerdes's stomach.

"Something heavier than dread settled in Xerdes's stomach."

Chapter 11
Death Mask

Trisday, 8th of Torgan
1856

The assassin's severed torso struck the tavern floor before Xerdes even saw the strike. He died with such a look of such shocked alarm that the thief was held there, staring into his clouding eyes almost hypnotically, until a sterling flash caught the lamplight at the side of his head, and he narrowly avoided joining him.

The Wraith was an agent of inviolate death. Swiping errantly right and left, a cinereal storm of slashing and spinning slaughter. With each savage stroke, limbs, heads, and other assorted body parts tumbled to the floor, as the murderous phantom continued on its undeviating path toward Xerdes. Already, the floorboards were so slick with the black blood of O'Nan's Afa assassins that the thief could scarcely find a foothold to whirl out of the way of his advancing assailant.

"Shirái..." Azin muttered, transfixed by the sight of his preordained doom.

He didn't have long to wait, as the very next strike separated his shoulders from his stomach, his body collapsing in sections as a splash of red stained the unbroken blackness of the slippery floor. Coin spilled in all directions from shorn pockets hidden all about his barkeep's apron, as if exploding from the bisected body itself. Xerdes, ducking off to the tavernkeeper's side, hauled himself up on to a nearby table and took hold of the rafters as a second slash narrowly missed his shins.

Pulling himself up into the roofbeams to evade his pursuer with a herculean effort, pain still lancing through his missing finger, Xerdes heard a ragged whisper tear from the phantom's throat as a stiff strike took the Wraith by surprise. Tián had buried his staff between what *might* have once been the thing's shoulderblades and sent it careening, off-balance, into a nearby beam. As his unspeaking Ferás-sûn companion closed the distance, the Wraith whirled upward, using the momentum of his tumble to erupt upward with a pitiless rapier strike. It nearly sheared through Tián's exposed arm, leaving a deep, carmine gash on his left bicep that spewed blood immediately. The Ferás-sûn did not even look down or acknowledge the wound. He didn't even wince. Sliding down into a balanced stance, he simply prepared to parry a second blow.

It was said the wolven people of the Alcaire forest were disciplined to such a degree that they felt no pain whatsoever while embroiled in the heat of battle.

Watching Tián, Xerdes felt comfortable confirming the rumor.

The second blow never arrived, however, as two hooded Afa assassins struck at the Wraith from both sides, sensing he was distracted. The deathly apparition simply whirled, slashing madly at both sides like a rising corkscrew. The Bord to his right lost both legs in the bargain, while black blood came sputtering out of the throat of his ally opposite. The nebulous, steaming liquid bathed the Wraith's ceramic mask, giving him an even more hellish aspect in the lambent light of the dimmed tavern.

He didn't bother to wipe it. There would be plenty more.

Sháiná, eyes wide with terror, scurried across the floor, her hands slipping periodically amid the bloodied floorboards. Leaving a deep black stain down the front of her plunging gown. The Wraith seemed entirely uninterested in her as she ran shrieking from the tavern, driven raving mad by the horrors of the abattoir where once had stood a tavern.

With the assassins and Azin's hired thugs dragging their fallen leaders through the doorway and disappearing in unqualified retreat, there were few remaining places for the wily thief to hide.

The Wraith knew it.

Turning to one of the wooden supports—the very *thin* wooden supports—the Wraith began mercilessly hacking away at them as Tián moved to stop him. The Ferás-sûn was instantly repelled by a perfectly placed kick that tore into his wounded shoulder and sent the wolven warrior sprawling across the blood-soaked floor. A silent scream tore from his useless vocal cords as his muzzle pursed in abject agony, pain at last registering on his previously impassive face.

The Wraith went to work, hacking away at the beam with a broadsword purloined from one of the fallen Afa. It didn't take long for it to splinter and buckle in as Xerdes crouched atop it and watched the bulbous roof seem to lean in even lower. Atop these underground

Nazgan-style dwellings an entire tenement perched. He wasn't overjoyed at the prospect of moving in the hard way.

With each strike, Xerdes had to steady himself on the rafters to avoid tumbling to the floor, and watched with mounting apprehension as the beam bent farther and farther inward, such that even the flames of the brazier-mounted torch tongued at the beam now looming above.

The torch which hovered precariously several feet above the Wraith.

As the assailant briefly exchanged his dulling and bent broadsword for a nearby hand-axe across the tavern, the thief seized his chance. Skittering across the rafters, he swung his entire body downward in a gymnastic swipe. His left boot tipped the torch from the brazier.

And catapulted it directly toward his hooded enemy.

Even soaked by the blood of dozens, the sackcloth-like cloak erupted like dried tinder. Something approximating panic gripped the thing, as it instinctively grabbed the hilt of its silver rapier and locked it in a deathgrip. But no blade would save him from the stinging flames. An ear-splitting scream tore from the wounded throat of the Wraith, and unable to free himself from the fabric wound about him... he catapulted headfirst through the front door and out into the street to extinguish the fire amid the fast-coming sandstorm.

Xerdes landed nimbly, still favoring his hand with the severed finger. He shook his head at a nearby bow and arrow, knowing archery was about as useful as lace pants in his current state. Then he leaned over to examine Tián. The wound was ominously deep, but with mending, he'd survive. At least in the expert medical opinion of a man who picks pockets for a living. Which he reckoned would be a new and inviting challenge after today.

Tián's head suddenly wrenched to the left, and for a moment, Xerdes thought he may be having a fit.

"Save the death throes for a more serious wound," he assured, "You'll live. If you call this living."

The Ferás-sûn shook his head and wrenched it to the left once more. Xerdes' brow furrowed as he followed his gaze. Across piles of inanimate bodies and pools of plasma.

To a blood-spattered object propped awkwardly against a nearby wall.

A smile crept across the thief's face as he realized what it was.

"Tián," he muttered, "I may have to keep you around after all."

DEATH MASK

The Wraith's screams gradually subsided, as the last of the flames were extinguished amid the sandswept streets of Kara'Zin. Awkwardly, the thing hauled itself unevenly to its feet, its singed fingers still clutching the hilt of its rapier.

Then it stumbled forward, as if propelled from behind, nearly falling in a heap.

The masked face, still stained with a single splash of obsidian blood, looked backward to see a single feathered shaft protruding from its shoulder. Framed in the tavern's doorway, Xerdes stood. One arm clutched to his side, still cradling his injured arm. In the other, he clutched a blood-caked crossbow.

Despite the wind, the street was so quiet, Xerdes could've heard a dagger slide between a pair of ribs two districts over.

"Xeeeeerdeeeees..." he heard the thing gurgle.

"One day," sighed the thief, "We're going to have a conversation where I don't have to play both parts."

Then, a bizarre thing happened.

He heard the rapier point stab suddenly into the earth. The Wraith's masked head cocked awkwardly sideways, as his arm reached up, over, and with a sickening pop, dislocated itself. Then, with eerie ease, the arm withdrew the crossbow bolt from his upper shoulder with a violent jerk. With that, it settled back down at a nauseating angle, and with another deafening pop, returned to dangle limply beneath the folds of the still-smoldering cloak, the bolt still hanging from its skeletal digits.

Xerdes reevaluated his prior hypothesis about this thing being human.

"Anái[1]," he mumbled, half conscious to himself, "...you can turn back up any time now."

With a wordless charge, the Wraith seemed to abandon all tactics, pulling his rapier from the ground, the blade tip dragging on the sodden ground behind him as he thundered toward the doorway. Xerdes would have paused to admire the irony of accidentally baiting his enemy into making the same mistake twice in one week, but he had

---

[1] **Anái:** Valen god of light and salvation. Like all the old gods, Valen orthodoxy maintains that, after creating the continent of Trávinas (the Westerlands) and turning back the forces of Darkness, they retired to the distant and unseen Easterlands, where they still slumber today.

only enough time to drop the crossbow and cartwheel from the doorway.

Framed stoically behind him, an arrow already knocked to a bow,
glowered Tián. The tip of the arrow was aflame. The tip of the arrow
was in flight.

The tip of the arrow was embedded in the Wraith's other shoulder.

The Wraith went up like dry hay. Only the gradually intensifying gusts
of dry wind stayed their intensity from erupting into an outright inferno.
By way of possible escape, Xerdes decided to extinguish them further.

' The thief spun, and all at once, a plume of searing sand he'd gathered
from the dusty streets erupted from his good hand, piercing the ceramic
slits where the Wraith's eyes had once peered out.

A guttural scream spilled from the spectre's unseen mouth. The silver
blade tumbled harmlessly from wrapped fingers as he wrenched the mask
free from his face and folded impotently to his knees.

Xerdes tumbled back upon the sand-strewn street and sat, statuesque
and frozen. Unable to look upon the face of the man whose identity had
already slowly dawned on him. Unable to lock that vengeful steel-gray
gaze, lean, pointed features long-disfigured by fire, torture or both...
distinguishable to the thief only by the head of longish hair still pulled
back tightly in a fencer's ponytail.

He shuddered and sank away from the mangled visage of the thing that
had been Davien Lucard.

"One does not survive a botched assassination..." the voice softly
gurgled. A long, jagged scar across what had been an elegant throat
explained why. "Without being accused of being... in league with the
target..."

"Is that what you're here for?" Xerdes halfheartedly intoned, "Hired
again to finish the job?"

A sardonic rasp that might have been intended as a chuckle served as
his initial reply. Even Tián's eyes fell to the ground as he moved to fill the
doorway of the tavern. A gesture of unspoken respect for a formidable
combatant.

"You... misunderstand. Your parasitic kind often do," the smoldering
thing gurgled.

"My kind are usually gone before there's a 'misunderstanding,'" Xerdes
replied, just boldly enough to almost turn his eyes from the ground.

"Youuuu…" the spectre said with effort, visibly cringing each time he parted his scarred lips, "Are a wanted man. The old crimelords' loss… was the new Underseers' gain…"

Xerdes went rigid at the word. If it were possible for anything to be worse than what he'd fled in Menuvia, the Underseers were it.

"…and I was the only hireling… to meet you… and survive. If inhabiting this… pitiful form can even be called survival…"

Xerdes said nothing but just managed to look his handiwork in the eye. He'd not left most of these wounds, though he logically discerned that the missing arm had been a gangrenous token of the shoulder wound he'd left him with during their combat. The scar tissue that crisscrossed the shattered and asymmetrical face, crooked knees and ankles splintered severely and never set during long hours of interrogation, and a remaining arm so heavily bandaged that he needn't speculate what horrors it concealed all relayed the story without any elucidation from what was now known as "the Wraith."

He spat at Xerdes' feet.

"Look upon it, thief," he said with a wince. "I was not *paid* to put an end to your idiocy…"

"…when they took my arm… they left *this*…" he indicated to the argentine weapon, "…just out of reach. If it was to taunt me… or from sheer hubris… I know not. Strapped to the rack so long… I learned how to…"

The painful effort of speaking overwhelmed him for a moment, and after a deep, dry swallow, he continued, "…I… dislocated my remaining arm… to gain enough reach… and then…"

Without wanting to, Xerdes found he gaped at his nemesis. The thief caught himself, but not quickly enough to stop Lucard from registering a morbid grin. The pain of the gesture had clearly been worth it just to watch Xerdes recoil in disgust.

"…they… became the first… of my victims."

Xerdes shook his head and punctuated the testimony, "…and if there's any truth to the tales out of Vale… I gather they weren't the last."

A grin that looked painful for even an unscarred face split across Lucard's wounded flesh as he rasped, "That honor… will be *yours*."

The Wraith collapsed forward, as if succumbing to his myriad wounds. For a moment, Xerdes started to breathe a sigh of relief. Until its momentum continued, rolling from its singed shoulder, toward where the rapier had fallen, drawing it up in a single, astonishingly acrobatic motion he had barely enough time to block with his dagger.

The blade catapulted from the thief's unsteady grasp and into the blotted-out sky. The Wraith lost no time, swiping ravenously sideways and down, barely catching the edges of the thief's ragged apparel as he darted backward and sideways, forward and downward. With unerring dexterity, Xerdes dodged the rapier point again and again, Lucard's strikes becoming wilder and more desperate as his blade failed to find purchase.

Davien Lucard was more dangerous, wounded and with one arm, than a battalion of fresh-faced and healthy infantry. But he was exhausted from his combat in the tavern and wounded near-mortally besides. He slipped to one knee as his attacks began to slow, still thrashing even as he sank, his face taking on the reddish purple of utter desperation and hatred.

Tián, who had not moved from the door until that point, suddenly pressed his right arm to his chest in a Ferás-sûn military salute. His chest lowered to the opponent in what appeared to be a slight bow.

Then he quietly traversed the street and took position behind Lucard.

He drew the dagger deeply and cleanly across the man's scarred throat, a torrent of scarlet blood spilling upon the sands as he did.

Xerdes looked up, his lungs burning, eyes bulging in surprise. He watched Tián mouth unspoken words as the corpse crumpled to the street.

Even without a sound, he could see the words were Aven in origin. He could only piece together one from watching what passed for Ferás-sûn lips.

"Hythái."

He hoped it meant something like "mercy."

The Ghostwind howled a dirgelike lament through the deserted byways of Kara'Zin, and the two friends found that they were alone with death.

Chapter 12
Epilogue

By the time Tián and Xerdes parted company, the radiance of the late afternoon sun had slackened. The dreamy, pre-twilight hours made the abandoned byways of Kara'Zin's Lirazá Quarter seem static and otherworldly. Xerdes had never seen deserted streets more alive. In the time they had spent in the company of Azin, the streets of Kara'Zin had been harried by a blustery tempest to rival the Ghostwind itself. A wall of opaque brown obscured all but what lay but a few feet before the thief.

Xerdes took firm hold of the Ferás-sûn's forearm, and they locked eyes in understanding.

Even if Tián had been capable of speaking, words would not have availed him above the howling wind. Then the thief pressed something into the palm of his newfound friend's hand. The stern, wolven head looked down and saw a beautifully crafted clasp, oversized and intricately detailed. One intended for a Horrand cloak. He began to proffer a quizzical look to his companion when the thief raised a single hand to still him.

"Something I don't need anymore" he mouthed amid the din.

With a solemn nod, Tián clipped the thing to his belt. Then the Ferássûn turned, wrapped one hand firmly around his walking stick and with a single wave, disappeared into the blustering whirlwind.

In the center of the beshrouded courtyard lay a marble fountain, carven in the long decades of L'Intaza rule. Whatever its native name was, he'd never discerned, but foreigners in the Alienage called it "the Sky Fountain." The previous regime had gone in for gaudiness, and the current one evidently agreed.

Deep veins of gold had been embedded in its artfully sculpted surface, and at its center was a solitary statue of a woman, half-nude, clad only in a flowing gown, which draped lazily from her left shoulder.

Xerdes looked up at the darkening sky and breathed deeply, heedless of the dust that promptly poured into his lungs. Even pelted by a flurry of fine sand, it was the most free he had felt in what seemed like ages.

Squinting into the distance, the stinging spray had just dissipated enough for the tip of the southeastern wall to be distinguishable beyond the domed housetops and through the slender spires of the Kara'Zin skyline. He tried not to notice that accursed rod-iron weathervane, molded into the shape of a naval compass whirling atop a distant rooftop. He tried to pretend he did not know precisely which roof it was perched upon.

Xerdes had devoted two decades to forgetting that thick oaken doorframe that loomed at the vestibule of the Orphanage. Kelvius it was called then. He didn't care what disconsonant briar of Bordish nonsense they were calling it now. He tried not to linger on the irony that the name they'd given him—Xerdes—was itself a disconsonant briar of Bordish nonsense.

When one finds a stray dog deposited on their doorstep, they rarely ask its opinion on what it should be called. "Not this far south of Highcrest, anyway," he thought, as he watched Tián fading down the dusty streets in the distance.

He dipped to wash his sodden face in the fountain and, at long last, closed his eyes.

I should never have come back, he thought.

Then his eyelids grudgingly parted, unfurling a pristine reflection in the water.

Though the air all about him had dimmed to a luminous brown, he began to distinguish shapes at the heart of the ruddy mistral.

The bronze sky became two eyes like blue ice. The faltering sunlight to cascading blonde ringlets. A pale, beautiful face peered knowingly back at him from the great abyssal beyond below the calm surface of the pond. Present, but never material. Feeling without form.

His breath ceased. He saw Saryss smile.

Whatever fell from his eyes, the Ghostwind winnowed away in a single brutal, buttressing gust.

When he gazed down once more, only the waters of the fountain stared back. The soft smile replaced with a still surface, as smooth as polished glass. Accompanied by a haggard reflection it took more than a moment to recognize as his own.

"Hela Nectar. 'A bargain among narcotics.'"

Xerdes repeated, almost believing it.

EPILOGUE

Tián was more than an hour outside of Kara'Zin when he at last braced himself against the roaring gale and reached for his leather canteen. As he did so, his wrapped hands brushed against the Horrand ornament that now dangled from his belt, as a reminder of his strange and brief acquaintance.

Even above the low howl of the Ghost Wind, a faint rattle resounded.

Pale gray eyes narrowed instinctively.

He detached the trinket from his belt and examined it, feeling something shift within as he did so.

Then he found a small protrusion on the far edge of the massive clasp, and pulling it free, the object split in half, lengthwise, down the center.

His wolven eyes widened.

In the hollow between both halves, hidden in plain sight, was a single coin of argent silver. The size of a man's fist.

Emblazoned with a silver hawk.

Appendix

A Valen Word on the Waylands, Volume I

*This being a comprehensive handbook and appraisal
of Vale, its surrounding territories and peoples*
---by---
Jerith Marcand
Recorder, Tirionus
18th Dögn, 1851

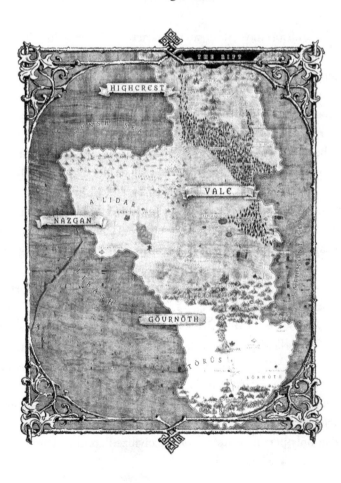

Trávinás

The Westerlands

By edict of our venerated King Relegant, the sanction of this document is as follows: To itemize each of the Great Powers of the continent of Trávinás in turn, and its populations. To delineate each in brief, with as keen an eye for objectivity as an ally or rival can hope to achieve. Finally, to provide contextual experience with a brief chronicle of each. It is this humble recorder's hope that in doing so, we provide the lettered inhabitants of Vale and visitors from abroad, with a more worldly perspective of lands they may be inclined or disinclined to visit. In so doing, it is believed we might foster more gregarious discourse with ally and otherwise, and facilitate mutually beneficial trade, thereby.

First and foremost, ever at the heart of Trávinás (or "The Westerlands," colloquially) has our empire's might stood stalwart. A buttress of enlightenment and civilizing influence against the changeable wiles of the waylands and their empires. We shall nevertheless forego judgment of those lands in favor of calculating fact whether said powers are allied or in opposition to our own. It is also true that other continents have been discovered, accounts of which vary wildly in credibility and content. For certain, during the great exploratory Age of Endeavor (1450–1690) Ánvinás was discovered by Horrand explorer/conqueror Pön Tellod across the sea of Akhrensk Nûr to the distant south. Rávinás to the north was discovered by Aven scouts many centuries prior, but geographic difficulties (primarily, those anomalies created by the Rift) made it virtually unexplorable until the radical advances in naval craft in the 15th century, and while we have heard various reports that it may have inhabitants, we can verifiably confirm little beyond this fact. Religious doctrine and myth in Highcrest and Vale has spoken extensively of the Easterlands far across the expansive Sea of Cathmont. Reports emerged in 1591 of a mythical land spotted by exhausted Aven parties, dubbed Sirvinás, (Eastland, in the Aven tongue) but the only survivor succumbed to exhaustion (and mysterious wounds) before she could sufficiently describe the sight or location. This account, therefore, will catalog only pertinent details of the civilized continent with which we are familiar: Trávinás itself.

As Imperial Recorder, I pray by all the Driváni slumbering, perhaps on that mysterious continent in the East, that the recent years of peace will facilitate that aim.

Section I
The Major Powers

What follows being a catalog of the principal
empires of Trávinás and their inhabitants

Vale: Cradle of the Continent
Men

DEATH MASK

"Industrious. Officious. Studious. Moral. Pious.
All these virtues and more, Men strive and fail to embody.
Vale is an eternal adolescent."

—*"A Nation Apart"* by Káevánás IV, 1441

No matter the region or its climate, wildlife, or fertility, Men seem always to propagate. Those who hail from specific regions may differ in skin or hair color. However, the continued presence of ubiquitous migration in recent years of peace and plenty has diversified the physical palette considerably. For example, the people of Menuvia (Vale's former capital) are known for being pale of face and dark of hair, their roots long believed to be intertwined with Aven stock. A popular belief—or delusion—among Menuvian nobility.

APPENDIX

Tirionus—being one of Vale's two capital cities—has a very diverse physical appearance, but the original settlers of the city were known for their red and brown hair and a complexion noticeably darker compared with those of the Menuvians. To the north and the west in the warmer climes of Romatho, even darker shades remain indigenous, many having hailed originally from the sun-scorched climes of neighboring Nazgan, while the fishing and foresting cities of Alegria, Tambria, and Aphelan have long had a reputation for attracting a diverse cultural set. Their original inhabitants were known for having almost uniformly brown hair and eyes, with a mid-toned pallor. These are, of course, generalities, and as peoples and cultures have pollinated the continent, such hard and fast rules are broken nearly as often as they are ratified.

The modern political face of Vale is characterized by the union of the Twin Capitals, which are seated a considerable geographic distance from each other. Ostensibly equal in authority and executive power; in practice, one compliments the other, thus retaining the delicate balance of the dual monarchies of Man. The capital at the center of Vale—and the seat of most political power—is Tirionus. It is a grand, majestic city that rose from the ashes of ancient Calmon after it was razed to the ground during the Cerulean Empire's reign of terror (1173–1202). Menuvia, the former capital, having surrendered to the Cerulean usurper king (whose accursed name need not be spoken), was not only divested of its status, but a second capital was selected to better diffuse governmental influence in the future. Senators from all over Vale come to the first of these twin capitals—Tirionus—to hold court and to petition the king for aid. In this year (1851), it is ruled by King Relegant, an amiable ruler, thoroughly seasoned and famed for his advocacy of the arts, literature, and music. Under his tutelage, Tirionus has become the envy of the continent, the symphonies of Merién and the jaw-dropping frescoes of Araelus replacing much of the military might of its blood-soaked past. Although politically adept, King Relegant is thus widely respected and admired among the people.

The second of these Twin Capitals is Sensenal, situated far to the southeast at the feet of the Agrigör Mountains, almost bordering the snowy crags of Göurnoth. It wields the industrial and production understructure of Vale, with its advantageous position beside rich mountain ore veins, which have proven productive without depletion for centuries.

DEATH MASK

The swarthy-faced Karnish Men dwell in the Sensenal region and for generations installed their own lords in seeming autonomy. The nearby shores of the Virandia River further compound Sensenal's embarrassment of natural riches. King Draylon is the present ruler of the shared imperial seat. He was well-acquainted with Lord Relegant as a child, and theirs is an iron-clad friendship, borne of mutual respect and shared values, if not always goals. For Draylon is a much younger man who is only now reaching middle age while Relegant, still heirless, is fast approaching his dotage.

For all Menuvia's reduced status, much of the financial and political power in Vale is still wielded in the Menuvian Senate, installed as a placative gesture after Menuvia was stripped of its place as capital of Vale, and publications of varying repute even now publish rumors that the halls of the senate have quietly begun to echo with whispers of conspiracy. Some might even describe this mad effort as a long-deferred attempt to reform the Menuvian military and to march on Tirionus to sue for concessions. Whatever its true nature, that the soaring oratory of the ambitious senator Bal-Ashid has found many a sympathetic ear is beyond doubt. Menuvia now flies its own banners openly, eschewing the Valen crossbrand as its standard. this is a show of autonomy and independence Lord Relegant has, in his wisdom, gracefully permitted without bloodshed.

Unwary waylanders should note that the official language of Vale is Talorn, and the names of cities of the region are taken from Talorn, while many of the Mannish names are also derived from it. It is largely educed from several more arcane sources, namely Lársólá[1] and Agrigör[2] but has taken on an idiosyncratic timbre of its own.

While Valen civilization has often found itself at war, both of overt military aggression (the Horrand Invasion, 1120–1123) and more subtle subversion (the Nazgani Intrigues, which spanned the 13th and 15th centuries in fits and starts), the cradle of Man finds itself in an extended period of peace and some less savory voices in the Menuvian Senate argue, more than a little geopolitical stagnancy. Far to the north, the

---

[1] **Lársólá:** Language of the Aviári and Ferás-sûn peoples.

[2] **Agrigör:** The now-dead language of the Horrand peoples.

APPENDIX

Aven Empire has withdrawn to its craggy kingdoms, no longer overtly vying for cultural or political rulership of the continent. The Horrands are once again fractious and imbibe in unchecked civil war, and though Nazgan seems always to whisper of conspiracy and invasion, explicit aggression has yet to emerge since King Brethal VIII withdrew the Imperial Army from the Bord kingdoms (without bothering to actually extract them, some mad conspiracy theorists allege).

Rightly or wrongly, it is believed that Vale's greatest threats foment within its own borders. Apart from portents of a possible Menuvian Republic movement, in Uplith and Romatho, a revolt of a separate kind has emerged among agricultural workers and non-citizen serfs. Patrician Lord Gregus Felroth—popular both among the court and the peasantry—has proven himself a capable mediator in the ongoing dispute, though clashes between the Guard and unruly serfs wielding a symbolic white banner remain sadly common.

Northern Highcrest: Throne of Creation

The Aviári

APPENDIX

"Göurnoth its sturdy feet,
Nazgan its long-reaching limbs,
Vale its beating heart,
Highcrest its punctilious mind."

—*Homilies of Canthador*, Various Authors, 706

From the earliest days of the Dawnlight Empire (yr. 1–570 [esti-mated]), our northern neighbors, the Aven people, have dwelled in the mountains of Highcrest. A verdant and craggy country. Seat of civiliza-tion and intrigue. Patron nation of art, architecture, and music.

What is seen within as a bastion of culture, both ancient and modern, it must be admitted can be regarded in the South as something approaching egotism and pretense.

Physically, they are not dissimilar from Men save that their features have a characteristic ivory pallor, and their hair color can vary from strawberry blonde to platinum and reputedly even to silver. Their gaze shines steely gray, light blue, or in a few cases, even pale gold. Their defining characteristic, however, is, naturally, the expansive wings upon their backs. In some cases, these prodigious appendages can span their body length plus one half. In adulthood, they are said to fly with ease, and their natural physical grace (Aviári tend to be quite thin and lithe as a people) only adds to the spectacle of more than one Aven lord in flight. Of their maturation, precious little is known in the South, though tales from periods of closer relation betwixt our people tell that they do not sprout their vaunted wings until adolescence, essentially keeping juveniles naturally grounded. Indeed, even when pubescent young adults become accomplished enough at holding themselves aloft that they are permitted entry to the world-renowned academies at Lyndenál[3], they are largely regarded as infants. One of many indicia of the Winged Ones' natural affinity for magic and the arcane.

They speak Lársólá, an ancient and melodious tongue that is quite del-icate sonically and has many unique rules and characters. (See: Lársólá:

---

[3] **Lyndenál:** A land mass which is reputed to hover high above the Highcrest Moun-tains. Making the winged pilgrimage to their highest summit is a rite of passage for both warrior and magical aspirant alike.

The Aviári Language) Their language is not as widely known as it once was, though many Talorn words and even a few Agrigörian phrases are derived from Aviári.

Favored of the Driváni, the Divine Creators of Long Myth who are said to have spawned all the people of the continent, colloquial superstition holds that when the divines retreated into the perilous East for their centuries-long hibernation, the favor they'd formerly afforded their first creation slumbered with them. It is said that the lingering remnant of this deific esteem is felt in their preternaturally long lives. While a Man may count himself fortunate to perish in his 9th decade, an Aven Man would only be reaching mid-life then. While we admittedly know little of the Winged Ones or their ways in the modern day, it is with little doubt that this Recorder opines that a citizen of the Aven Empire passing before his 100th year would be marked by most as a premature tragedy.

From Yr. 1 of the common reckoning to the 7th century—over half of the first millennia on this continent—the Dawnlight Empire of the Aviári enjoyed uninterrupted dominion over the explored continent. By the turn of the 8th century, however, the decline of the Aven Empire could no longer be denied. Every face in the Archcouncil blanched when King Lóreális (681–741) spoke the nameless horror aloud during a public address. Though his intent was to steel the resolve of his people, he unwittingly gave form to their latent anxieties. Though the Aviári would grow in territory over the coming centuries, in many ways, the applicable power of the empire never truly recovered. By the time Menuvian Hero-King Torian referred to the Aviári as the "Twilight Empire" in his 850 Laytide Address, the ailing Aven nation was too despondent to even rebuke the evident insult. The Mannish middle-child had outshone the favored firstborn of the Driváni.

As bright as the whitest spires in Highcrest, their shadows are darker still. A history of imperial ambition, oft achieved through subjugation and enslavement (as its tribal neighbors, the Ferás-sûn can readily attest), and not-infrequent conflicts with Men and Horrands have chilled its reception with so many other peoples of the western continent that at least two of the major powers of Trávinás (Göurnoth and Nazgan) no longer treat diplomatically with the Aven Empire with any regularity.

Perhaps most unsettling is that the Aviári do not seem to mind. Willingly retreating to their mountain holds and the floating citadel to jealously guard their occult secrets and horde, the product of perhaps the richest culture the continent has ever seen. Indeed, some small towns in Vale and Göurnöth have a citizenry that simply doesn't believe that the Aviári even exist. (This humble recorder, for his part, can very much confirm that they do, having personally transcribed numerous diplomatic affairs between Tirionus and Válieri.) It has been hundreds of years since Men, Horrands, or even the Aviári's nearest neighbors, the Ferás-sûn, have interacted with their society in any politically meaningful way.

The trinary culture of the Aven Empire is split among three principle territories:

I. The Válieráns

𝕾𝖁𝕾(𝕰)

The Válieran bloodline, which claims royal root, is, as the name suggests, centered in the Aven capital of Válieri. Theirs is a more worldly, largely flightless society, more concerned with urban excess and enjoying the fruits of a decaying empire than becoming embroiled in world affairs or venerating Aven tradition. A stunning indulgence, for the city that houses the throne, but it goes some way to explaining the state of current affairs in Highcrest. It would, however, be a mistake to dismiss the Válieri line as wholly ineffectual. The Tythái Order, a sect of spies par excellence throughout the continent, stems from Válieran stock.

II. The Lóriális

𝕾(𝕰)𝖁𝕾𝕾

The Lóriális line, whose epicenter is the central hold of Highcrest city itself, is a more secular reflection of the Aviári that once were: the society that built its empire as much with diplomacy and relations as with martial might and taxation. Most Aven who venture from Highcrest's borders today are of Lóriális stock, and given their reputation in the South for arrogance and introspection, one wonders at the dizzying depths to which the remainder of their empire has degenerated.

III.   The Lyndenáli

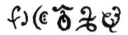

Finally, the Lyndenáli line, which represents the archmages, warlocks, and sorcerers of Aven society, of which there is a shrinking pool. Theirs is a more inward-looking and elitist line of patrician bearing and military skill. Much of Man's quarrels with the Nation of the Wing has, in fact, been a proxy conflict at the behest of the Lyndenáli sect. Aviári who demonstrate aptitude with harnessing the entropy of the arcane, upon attaining flight, may soar to the eternally hovering fortress of Lyndenál, (an unnatural phenomenon theorized to be the result of some sorcerous rite gone horrifically wrong [See: 'Lyndenál, Hovering Horror', 1331]) there to unravel the ancient and profane secrets of the People of the Wing.

Yet while the degrees of observance differ among the lines, the Aviári are without exception a society in which manners and class are paramount. They have a sort of unspoken caste system whereby the nobility are naturally more privileged while the underclasses have their needs provided by an extensive, if overtaxed, governmental welfare program. Reports of varying levels of repute suggest that there has been increased socio-political strife within the Aven Empire in recent years, with the underclasses coming nearly to violence on more than one occasion, leading some Aviári politicians to contend that they should be taking a more active role in international affairs. If for no other reason than to distract the idle ears of the Aven populace from the whispers of sedition.

Southern Highcrest: Womb of Wakening

The Ferás-sûn

DEATH MASK

"A beast at war is predictable. Its instincts chart a discernible, if destructive, course. A beast at peace is a fluctuant and inscrutable thing. As like to acquire a taste for the flesh of its own as for its neighbors."

—Náithá, Aven Military Strategist, 1291

The forest-dwelling Ferás-sûn, a clannish, pastoral society, are a stoic and self-sufficient race. Each tribe is an entity unto itself. Yet each strives to pull these loose collectives together into something resembling cohesion. Virtually the only fully united aspect of Ferás-sûn society (such as has been attained) is their language, which Valen archivists have at least discerned is a regional, heavily accented variant of Lársólá, the language of their former Aven masters. Much of their early history is mired by repeated episodes of slavery and servitude, culminating in the unexpected rebellion of runaway-slave-turned-folk-hero Ántólás. Whatever actuality of his life has been lost to the mists of antiquity, modern scholars seem to concur that it was Ántólás who first united the tribes for their long-overdue liberation, and that it was also under his reign that they began to segment into the regional and cultural collectives we observe today. Reliable sources confirm this continued effort at tribal unification is commonly referred to as "Leáthárá." The secrecy of this nomenclature is matched only by the antipathy most rank-and-file Ferás-sûn hold toward the concept. They value family and tribe nearly as much as the near-sainted memory of Ántólás himself.

Recent expeditions to the Forest of Alcaire have confirmed the presence of five great tribes (or wûlóka in the Ferás-sûn dialect) though it is common knowledge even at our geographic and cultural remove that there are many dozens more, most of whom are nomadic or of negligible size.

I must state again my regret at the absence of "good" (read: verifiable) information on the Ferás-sûn, their culture, and their ways. Yet, sadly, their insular nature and distrust of waylanders makes this effectively inevitable, even among the few of these clans that regularly commune with the great powers of the continent.

Yet here is a brief description of these five great Wûlóká so well as it is in my power to record it. We shall begin in the land wherein they are believed to have originated: Highcrest.

APPENDIX

I. The Shriá

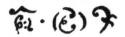

A warrior tribe linked directly to Ferás-sûn folk hero Ántólás himself, who named the clan after his first daughter. Though the group was founded on principles of wûlóká unity, they take their own clan's identity exceptionally seriously, and more than once have been credibly accused of undermining productive attempts at Leáthárá unification. It was the Aviári who laid blame upon The Shriá for the Ferás-sûn entering the War of the Rift (929–985) at such a late juncture. How the Winged Ones would have come upon this unconfirmed knowledge without rampant spycraft is a matter of speculation and conspiracy.

They answer to a single Kálá—effectively an absolute tribe leader—who in turn operates according to the guidance of the eldest of the Shriá, though the elder has no formal authority.

The Shriá's society venerates their mutual heritage and cherished military victories (for it was the Shriá who first codified many of the Ferás-sûn martial arts that led to many such triumphs) while the elder is responsible for relaying, and more recently, recording such deeds in writing for posterity. Unlike many other clans, the Shriá maintain regular contact and trade with the Aviári, however discreet. The Shriá occupy much of Kathylón and the surrounding Alcaire Forest, and it is through this central location that they are afforded greater influence, perhaps, than any other existing clan.

Their colors tend to be more akin to their brother timberwolves: a grayish mix of brown and red with unique markings owing to family lineage (hence why at official functions, back pelts are displayed openly as a sort of ceremonial dress uniform).

II. The Ákálár

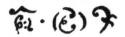

A staunchly pacifist tribe where suppression of interventionist political ideas borders on the very violence they purport to avert through such actions. Surprisingly, they are open to, if somewhat ambiguous toward, the concept of Leáthara. Their territory comprises a series of simple Tiáx villages that serve as a sort of suburb of Kathylón, surrounding much of its western edge.

Unanimity is the prevailing doctrine of their organizational structure with a six-member council of the most learned making every important decision for the Ákálár as a whole.

Similar in appearance to the Tûnáni, their coloring tends to skew somewhat redder and more yellow. Somewhat smaller than other tribes on the whole, they have acquired a reputation for using stealth, subterfuge, or diplomacy to acquire the same ends others would achieve through more offensive action.

III.   The Viren

Strictly beholden to the ideal of Ántólás despite lacking the direct claim to his ancestry enjoyed by the Shriá, although harboring deep convictions among its notoriously opinionated clansmen, it is nevertheless difficult for the Viren to legitimately challenge anything they find diplomatically objectionable. They have over time surrendered themselves to an oft-repeated parable (somewhat dubiously credited to Ántólás in 'The Battle Cry' (991), a tome of pithy quotations whose authorship is a subject of continued dispute) that if Leáthárá is not peacefully achieved after a period of two thousand years, the Átárná[4] will either return the forest-dwellers to the simple forms of their four-legged brethren the wolves... or snuff them out as punishment.

This macabre providence, preached by Viren mystics for centuries, has come to be called "Wenón ny Hile" (Roughly translated: "the Lost Past").

The Viren dwell in the highlands and woods along the banks of the Aldingwatch River, and, as such, have a distinct beige coloring often

---

[4] **Átárná:** The divine creators of the woods reputed to have awakened sentience in the Ferás-sûn.

characteristic of riverbank-dwelling wildlife with unique dark brown markings that easily distinguish between kin.

IV. The Tûnáni

For all the Shriá's ties with the Aven kingdom, the most "worldly" of the Ferás-sûn by far are the Tûnáni. Although they dwell in Tunwood—well outside Aven or Valen borders—there were Tûnáni living and trading openly in the human city of Torian and the Aven capital of Válieri for hundreds of years, forging lifelong bonds with the outside world that often make them outcast amongst their own. This was facilitated by their knowledge of fletching and woodcrafts, a constant demand for which exists in many major cities throughout the continent. By many of their fellows, they are therefore seen as corrupted and thus regularly stigmatized in Aldingwatch and Kathylón in their many recorded travels.

When history has credited the Ferás-sûn with open participation in matters of the world... their emissaries are invariably of the Tûnáni. It should come as little surprise, then, that the Tûnáni are, in turn, the most vocal in pushing for further inroads into the affairs of Aviári and Men.

The Tûnáni are known for being more foxlike in appearance with reddish cherrywood coloring and pointed features while still retaining the overall proportions of the more wolven tribes.

V. The Kiá

The only major clan that dwells outside of Highcrest or Vale are the Kiá. Dwelling on the frigid tundras of Göurnoth, their existence is a nomadic one from necessity, as they have followed the Cröd herds for generations. Also owing to their environment, the Kiá make a stark visual contrast from their forest-dwelling brethren. Their coats most often are white or gray (though black coats are an occasional occurrence among all Ferás-sûn), and their eyes are a pale gray or blue, perhaps another trait afforded by their chosen clime.

It is unknown how they came to be separated from the other wûlókás, but certain of my contemporaries offer two popular explanations: either as having been stranded during counterattacks at the height of the Horrand/Ferás-sûn War (986–991) or inferring some connection to the ancient seafaring ways of the early Viren clan, who even today regularly navigate the treacherous rapids of the Aldingwatch with unique ease. The first Horrand sightings of the Kiá called them "snow wraiths," for due to their isolation, location, and shocking appearance, many witnesses (in varying states of inebriation) assumed them some manner of ghost. That many of these earliest sightings came at the reputedly haunted ruin of Hardoval doubtless lent to such fancy.

Understandably stoic in their self-imposed isolation, in recent years, reports of Kiá representatives in attendance at wûlóká gatherings have gradually become more common. A likely reason for this sudden embrace of their fellow clans would be their frequent clashes with Horrands over resources such as Cröd, Gör, and Tragimi herds. Such conflicts with the natives have led to the Kiá's reputation as fierce and disciplined warriors.

From this haphazard conglomeration of miniature sub-societies, it should come as no surprise that the Ferás-sûn have no central government as we in the South would recognize it.

Renowned as peerless archers, scouts, and yeomen, the Ferás-sûn are also infamous for the eerie rumors of bizarre spiritual practices which emphasize the complete suppression of emotion. Ferás-sûn shamans teach all warriors an ancient rite called Sáidán, which is believed to be essentially a practice of storing up all fear and negativity experienced in battle and even daily life, and in a weekly ritual, expel it all at once. It is a sacrosanct undertaking that the Ferás-sûn have traditionally never allowed foreigners to witness, for it leaves them understandably vulnerable.

Ferás-sûn most commonly live in hollowed-out Tiax trees, a thick, stocky and internally-spacious species of tree native to the forests of

Highcrest. They install doors at their base, and carve out living compartments are found deep between the roots, which provide natural accommodations due to their tendency to spread laterally across the upper ground rather than downward as with many other phylums of plant. This provides a convenient natural foundation for the Forest Tribes' unique subterranean dwellings.

Separate, free, and self-assured, the Ferás-sûn are fast allies and fearsome foes. Lone wolves, newly unfettered.

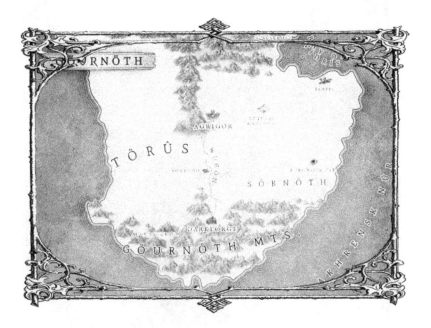

Göurnoth: Forge and Crucible

The Horrands

"The only time Göurnoth is not at war is when they are planning one."

—Lady Váriá (Disputed Quotation)

APPENDIX

To the distant south of Vale's borders, across the snowswept tundras of Törûs and spanning the vast, frigid coasts of Akhrensk Nûr to the south and east, lay the Anvil of Origin. Göurnoth. Hearth and home to the hardy Horrand folk, who for over 2,000 years have defied the might of merciless blizzards and feral beasts native to their icy abode to survive and thrive in defiance of all. This is in spite of their clannish ways and penchant for indiscriminate violence against friend and foe alike. Horrand society has no king, only a Firth, a kind of universal warlord who must perpetually defend his position from potential challengers among the Thörgs (Clans or Great Houses, in Mannish terms). Horrand society is one of eternal combat, shifting allegiances, and broken alliances.

The Horrand kräga (what Men might dub a kind of barbarian knight), who emerged in the 2nd century, both address, and typify, this ethos of self-sufficiency. they are roving, weapon-sworn warriors sometimes on friendly terms with, but never truly 'owned' by, any Firth or Thörg. Perhaps in reaction to this fractious culture, Kräga remain true only to one of the three immortal ideals of Horrand society, to which they swear a blood oath, and thereafter devote the entirety of their worldly endeavors:

I. Jägen

ノ ヽ ト 日 ↑ λ

Constancy is a virtue often sworn to the agrarian or mercantile inclined and repudiates laziness, inscrutability, or inconsistency for the nobility of exceptional craft. Few Kräga are sworn to Jägen as a virtue, for it lends itself more to workmanship, though those warriors that do are more often devoted to a single specialty discipline, such as swordsmanship or archery. Jägen-sworn marauders make ideal combat support, as they stubbornly refuse to withdraw, sometimes even under direct orders, and entire campaigns have been salvaged at the eleventh hour by one or two defiant companies of Jägen-sworn Kräga standing their ground in the face of overwhelming odds and emerging victorious.

II. Pötho

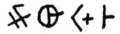

Justice, and those sworn to it, are a valuable commodity in the out-
lying communities, where local Thörgs are too preoccupied with petty
colloquial squabbles to lend the soldiery to their vassals. Its counterpart,
Khö (Vengeance), is forbidden but said to still be quietly practiced by
a few nameless Kräga who have nothing left to lose and a vendetta to
settle.

III. Thörgen

Loyalty is perhaps the most valued of all virtues among the Horrand
people. For all their warlike ways, they are also familial, merry, and
hospitable. Those Kräga who work under a clan tend to be sworn to
Thörgen.

Controversially, in 952, Firth Thoreg Förgnar added a fourth, Khanth,
or Altruism, which messengers inform us is more strictly observed as
legitimate in the South, near the capital, than in the Northern steppes of
Agrigör. More contentious still, the Service-sworn were overwhelmingly
military and solely allegiant to Förgnar himself, leading to accusations
from other clans that he had used the state war chest to muster his own
private army. Clashing philosophically as it does with the independence
of the Kräga, it is and was understandably unpopular among much of
the non-enlisted warrior class, and for a time, open battle between
the Firth's own military and the assembled legions of Kräga was common.

In Vale, Horrands are sometimes referred to as mountain men or
barbarians. In truth, they are closest to Men in physical proportion.
Yet that is where the similarities come to an abrupt halt. Horrands, on
average, stand several heads taller than an average Man. Reaching the
height of nearly one-and-a-half Men in some exceptional cases. Even

their women stand the height of the average Valen Man, but are quite often taller. Which is not to say that they are a particularly lean race. Quite the opposite. Horrands, both male and female, are known for their muscular, thick, and stocky builds. Their legs, in particular, are quite thick, ideal for braving Göurnoth's endless carpet of sleet and snow. As a result, they are a stalwart people, virtually without equal in combat. Were it not for their clannish and solitary culture, it is long surmised that no nation could stand against a united Horrand assault. During the brief periods where the Göurnoth nation was united under one banner— often one of tyranny—no deadlier force had ever been arrayed. Indeed, the Ferás-sûn, the Aviári, and even the Valen Empire of Men have all fallen to the combined might of a united Horrand military, (See: 'The Age of the Hammer', 1294–1450) though due to inexperience and disunity at the art of prolonged conquest, all three occupations were admittedly brief.

Horrands speak Talorn (the Mannish tongue), as a rule, which has been the case since Men won back their independence after the Razing of Uplith in 1291. Agrigör (or Agrigörian, as it is known in Vale), their ancient tongue, was discouraged by the human regents that ruled over Göurnöth at the time, so the people came to learn how to hide their true nature from their enemies. Indeed, rumors still persist of drunken Horrands all over Vale suddenly flying into Agrigörian verse or uttering ancient chants, so it may well be that the language is still very much alive, as some scholars have come to suggest.

The capital city of Göurnöth—occupied by a sovereign Firth—lies deep in the sprawling southern coastal mountains, in a grand city called DarkForge by Men. Few Horrands consider it their capital, and in-deed, few Horrands consider the Firth to be their ruler either. The Thörgs (or clan leaders) live and rule closer to home, and it is more often to they that a Horrand warrior swears his allegiance. There are two real societies in Horrand culture: those independent and enter-prising folk who survive in the mountains and tundras near the former capital of Agrigör and those in the southern portion of the country, nearer the proper capital of DarkForge. These two strata are sepa-rated as much by ideology and temperament as they are by geogra-phy, and their eternal struggle between dissolute government and absolute statism tells the tale of Göurnoth itself while the rank-and-file Horrands look on with some indifference. Some fishing villages lie far to the northeast in Jarvis, for example, but these cities are so remote and self-contained that they rarely interact with Göurnoth as a whole.

The darkest aspect of the Horrand psyche is shrouded in as much secrecy and myth as eyewitness confirmation. Battlefield tall tales, told by the firelight in Valen taverns aplenty, relay the story of Horrand warriors, teetering near death, punctured by innumerable arrows and bleeding from a dozen or more sword strikes, suddenly reddening, enlarging, swelling in physical size, and like a living battering ram, charging the enemy ranks intend on unremitting slaughter. In centuries past, the word that reached Valen ears for this phenomenon was Khötodor, though no scholar of Agrigör has yet revealed to me its import. (The root word Khö, as we have learned previously, means "vengeance," and as such, we may assume its likely meaning)

What few reliable accounts emerge of this Horrand bloodwrath are disquieting, however incredulous they may be. More than the mere berserker rage reported by some Valen warriors in the heart of battle and at death's door, the Horrand physically transmogrifies, with some even suggesting that their physical appearance takes on an "animalistic aspect." (Carpides, *Solitude and Savagery: Of the Mountain Men of Agrigör*, 481) Whatever its physical manifestation, the aftermath is marked in many reliable historical accounts: The Horrand is left dead, or so near it that he or she perishes in the aftermath, invariably surrounded by massacred foes. The Kräga feature heavily in such tales, as do their feminine counterparts, the Warmaidens of Göurnoth.

Whatever hidden power suffuses the icy blood of the Horrands, they are a formidable foe when sufficiently organized. Fortunately for human civilization, Horrands seldom are.

Nazgan: The Sandswept Snare

The Bords

"Can we do nothing of Karathis? Centuries of progress, culture and industry undone by a rodentine race of cutthroats and nomads!"

—Admiral Ethiet Ogden, *Collected Letters*, 1850

My scholastic integrity will permit me no other utterance in spite of this document's intended audience: There is no more suspicious or

APPENDIX

duplicitous a culture than the Bords. Dwelling in the arid desert plains of Nazgan far to the west, the fight for survival in their harsh climes is mirrored in their culture and political landscape.

The physical appearance of the Bord peoples sets them immediately apart. They are short, lean, and quick. Reptilian in nature, their skin is dotted in green or brown scales, and their eyes are little more than black slits, as of a snake. Their brow is low and thick, and their mouths are filled with razor-like teeth and long, forked tongues. They stand slightly hunched forward in an almost apelike posture, resting their weight on elongated forearms, never relying wholly on their much smaller hind legs. Their forearms being long as they are, Bord fashion often emphasizes this characteristic. Armguards, bracers, bracelets, gloves... all are staples of Bord apparel, and each one is more ornate than the last. For the Bord people have a love of fine embroidery, rich fabrics, and detailed intaglios which wind their way up even the tallest Bord structures.

Nazgan is an empire of thieves. Even their crown jewel, the capital city of Kara'Zin, is stolen. Making the matter more tender, still, is that this theft occurred quite recently, and at the cost of thousands of Valen lives.

It is no secret that the so-called nation fashioned by the Bords is quietly referred to as the "Traitor Kingdom" within Valen borders. For the Bordish people were once mere petulant upstarts, dwelling nomadically in the dunes and mountains north and east of Karathis, the most distant desert outpost of the Valen Empire. Though they already boasted a loose governmental structure in the mountain settlements the Valen legions have yet to chart, or even name, it was only in the 17th century that this reptilian race began to codify into one unified collective, ruled by a single Salár, who presided over a reasonably organized—if slipshod—military force. Há'Rihats (1625–1664) was the first of these to deal diplomatically with Vale in any material regard, and recorders of the time rate the interaction as amicable, if cool. His assassination at the hands of Thief Queen Zi'Án (a perfectly legitimate exchange of power in Bord tradition) marked the beginning of hostilities. Under her regime—perhaps even *directed* by it—Bords emigrated to Karathis by the thousands in search of succor. The reason given was a famine in the northern mountains of Nazgan, where the Bords had dwelt for centuries. In the aftermath of what followed, the near-simultaneous depletion of a half dozen silver mines would be revealed as the true culprit. Initially amenable to their needs, Valen King Shorvius accommodated the relocation. Karathis was, at this time thriving due to its own recently discovered silver and Helá deposits. Kings Caedran II and III ignored Nazgan entirely, and with Caedran III's death at the Rift Siege of Válieri in 1816, nearly two-thirds of the population of Karathis were of Bord ancestry. When Brethal VIII assumed the throne, many were already calling the century of emigration and displacement "the Quiet Conquest."

It was then that the Bords enacted their plan.

Wandering from the deserts in 1816, the nomad kingdom fell upon the outpost in numbers that made defense all but impossible.

A succession of bloody struggles between the Karathis garrison and the Bords under command of the wily but aging Salar Ráhánji, who had once again banded the nomadic Bords together for the gambit, ultimately led to the expulsion of Valen envoys from the region. Wisely, the Bords timed their assault to coincide with the death of King Caedran III, which was in the heart of the sweltering Nazgan summer. The Empire's reinforcements were nearly halved by the time the treacherous wastes of the A'lidar Desert were crossed.

With Valen legions falling en masse to the Bord invaders and guerillas in their own streets, the regent of Karathis expected the empire would send further reinforcements. Little did he know the empire was locked in a drama of succession following the king's death and, having been repelled by the Aviári, had no stomach for further military misadventure.

Karathis fell in the first month of 1817, and the newly installed King Brethal VIII—too distracted by the withdrawal from Highcrest—allowed it. It was thereafter named Kara'Zin. And the Salár who had organized the usurpation installed as a functional king. In the west, he (or she) is still routinely referred to as the Lord of Thieves for just this reason.

The many conflicts between our nations notwithstanding, Bord civilization is known the world over for its expertise in the arts of mercantile, painting, sculpture, and innovations of industry. Much of the modern mining technology adopted in our own country is inherited, or more often traded, from Bord designers. Societally speaking, influence, power and monetary riches, which despite its arid climate, can be found in abundance in Nazgan, are shared, and warred for, by several enduring strata of Bordish society. The most prominent of which are represented by the following quartet:

I.   The Zi'Zin Temple

ﺗﺞ ٩ ﻟ ﺗﺞ ٩ ﺗﺞ

   One of the few immovable constants in the shifting sands of Nazgan, it is no wonder even the oft-materialistic Bords place such faith in this enduring, if embattled, institution.   A nomadic folk by origin, Bord religious practices were similarly disparate in the many "wandering centuries" when their fellows roamed the dunes in search of trade, water, and wealth.   Since settling in Kárá'Zin, the 6 of these major faiths have been subsumed by the one Zi'Zin faith. Originally a cult of sun worship, in time, the sun took on a more sentient divinity.   In Vale, we know their one God as Zi'Zin, for the Bords have never revealed his or her name to outsiders, so we simply use the name of their temple itself when a name is required. Bordish society places particular significance on the utterance of names, believing a portion of their being to be contained therein. In their travels abroad, Bords will often assume an entirely separate nomenclature, intended for the tongues of waylanders alone. They retain the utterance of their name solely for family, friends, allies, or those of their inner acquaintance.   To the Bords then, to speak the name of their anonymous lord is an act of worship itself and to guard and defend it from the ears of outsiders the ultimate act of faith.

   With massive membership, marked by routine, devout worship (and the monetary offerings that come with it) the Zi'Zin Temple of 19th-century Nazgan is a political entity to rival and eclipse virtually any institution on the continent, including Kara'Zin's own government. As Nazgan's cloak and dagger history attests, any Salár that fails to reckon with the influence of the Zi'Zin priests will find it impossible to prosper and unlikely to continue to breathe.

II. The Mi'Mhád

ᚼ᚜᚟ᚼᚱᚾᚴ

To call the Mi'Mhád a mere merchant's guild is underselling the import of the enterprise. The Bords were once a naturally fractious and nomadic race. To collectivize Kara'Zin industry—from street vendors to silver tycoons—was a prodigious task and its execution an act of unbridled will and more than a little avarice. The Mi'Mhád, by necessity, became among the most ruthless conglomerates in the already-contentious polit-ical landscape of the Thieves' City. With more than one dozen warring mining and mercantile concerns, Bordish silk merchant K'lázh began to recognize the need to streamline as a means to preclude the incessant struggle between the competing interests.

Over the next half century, opponents were bribed, beaten, incen-tivized, and slain until at last but one entity emerged from the morass: the Mi'Mhád. The economic engine of Kára'Zin, no sect of Bordish society can even consider any major coup or acquisition without first considering how it might prevail upon the sensibilities of the merchant class. The Mi'Mhád are both the blazing sun and the dark cloud, looming over every other power in Kára'Zin.

III. The Afá

ᚱ ᚦ ᚱ

"Only in Kara'Zin would thievery be legal," goes the Eastern axiom. Functionally speaking, however, *nothing* is legal in Kara'Zin without the explicit consent of the Áfá. Cutthroats, thieves, assassins, and ganglords, any and all thrive in the Traitor Kingdom, its representatives and bosses citing the centuries-old practice of Bordish nomads legitimizing—and even venerating—such profligate conduct.

The Áfá have little need to camouflage their operations. They meet with the Sálár openly, in court, before civilians and courtiers alike. The Sálár may—and has—commission a killing, a theft, or an act of open aggression against anyone in his domain, and no Bordish legal statute would ever preclude it. Quite the opposite, the only way to face legal reprisal of any kind is if the act is *not* conducted openly before credible witnesses. Such contracts are called Thi'Ni, and they are the beating heart of Kara'Zin's underworld, which thrives as a direct result of this formal arrangement.

Far from attempting to remain covert, the Áfá and their many sub-groups and agents must be carefully documented and cataloged, and attempts are made to immediately approach and enlist (or remove) any independent who encroaches upon their domain.

IV. Jeh'Mhár

𐌉𐌂𐌆𐌋𐌅𐌆𐌽𐌕

The nobility of Kárá'Zin was established long before the usurpations of the Bords. Valen nobles—supporters of the regent both financially and influentially—served as a sort of patrician political class for centuries of Kara'Zin's early history. An unspoken (and unelected) soft Senate formed when the nobles' traditional social clubs began to take on an ever-more-political aspect, culminating in the formalization of the Kara'Zin Council. When the Bords seized the city as their own, this council (and the nobles within it) was too wealthy and influential to remove outright. It was renamed L'Intáza—a name we have never translated yet which is wielded as an insult among the Bordish nobility—and gradually divested of powers, territory, and influence.

In their place, industrious Bords began to collate their own K'ras Council, which today represents the public's only direct conduit to the leadership of Kara'Zin and widely seen as second only to the throne of Nazgan itself. It was less than a century before the Jeh'Mhár supplanted the L'Intaza as the wealthiest citizens, and soon these Valen nobles were finally deposed. A deal having been struck between the Jeh'Mahar and the priests of the Zi'Zin Temple to oust them by any means. A series of historically violent earthquakes across Nazgan, which the Zi'Zin credited as a consequence of the "godless" L'Intaza nobles, provided pretext. Their lands and holdings were seized and redistributed among the Jeh'Mahar and the merchants of the Mi'Mhád.

The Jeh'Mhár may be the canniest, and most connected, of all the power brokers in Kara'Zin.

Bord politics revolve primarily around the delicate dance between the Salár, the Bord nobility, the Mi'Mhád (Merchant Guild), the Afá (the legitimate face of the criminal underworld), and the Zi'Zin Temple, represented by the K'Zán. For any one element to fall out of balance risks the collapse of the young empire. To her credit, thus far, the Salár has walked this tightrope ably. Time will tell if her stride is sustainable.

The bulk of Bord commoners reside in slightly raised, underground dwellings, the circular ceilings packed with dirt to cool it from the sweltering elements of the A'lidár Desert, while the nobility content themselves with soaring spires of strikingly ornate masonry. Upon conquering Kara'Zin, the Bords reconstructed the entire skyline so that it now bears only the most tangential resemblance to the Valen stronghold of Karathis. Only the weathered walls of the metropolis, built by the Valen Elite Guard in millennia past, betray that secret.

The language of the Bords, Izákás, is widely believed to be among the most ancient tongues in known civilization, yet very little of it is understood by outsiders. While the nomadic early years of the Bord people have left it complex to a fault and cumbersome to use, it is nevertheless spoken by the entire nation of Nazgan, and even the most dedicated of Vale linguists and historians have yet to unlock its most jealously guarded mysteries, much like the deserts of Nazgan itself. By way of example, it was not until as recently as ten years ago that Tirionus scholars were able to compile a complete Izákás alphabet. (See: Izákás: the language of the Bords)

Perhaps the finest summary was penned by Davin Hilius, former Lord Regent of Karathis:

"The only way to truly know the Bords is to be one."

The Underkingdom of Mordas: Unknown or Apocrypha?

The Delvers

"We have charted every sea. Mapped every shore. The Aviári have even gone some way toward reckoning with the heavens themselves. But the deep, black places of the world remain a shadowy enigma."

—Julius Varcannian, *"The Age of Endeavor Ongoing"*, 1720

This scholar deliberated for many days and nights whether to include this section in the accompanying text at all, for the fallacious reports of a civilization residing in sprawling cavern complexes—the largest of these mythically named Mordas—beneath Vale and Göurnoth and even spanning the deserts of Nazgan outnumbers those from any credible source by a considerable amount. What decided the matter at last was the account from Tarius Varon (1306–1358), whose work I have much regard for and who claimed to have had a personal encounter—several, in fact—with a trade emissary from this reclusive race.

What he described is quizzical, sometimes even dismissed as the blatherings of a madman (for Varon perished prematurely of Parson's Kyloma some 7 years after the alleged encounter). For this scholar's part? I have thoroughly researched Varon's life and found that he presented no cognitive symptoms of the disease until 1356, meaning that he possessed his full faculties when it is purported to have occurred. So I will simply transcribe it and leave the reader to decide (with apologies, should a diplomat from such a society one day encounter this text and find it in any way inaccurate).

"...it was while wayfaring among the crags of Agrigör, bound for the smithy village of Blackcroft, that I chanced the unconventional route described by a bard in a tavern I'd passed two weeks previous. This "short-cut" claimed the presence of a little-known switchback trail intended for laden horses or domesticated Tragimi, once frequented by Karnish miners to move ore more expeditiously north to sell at the Valen markets (where the markup was substantial and more than covered the cost of the journey). Though it was only late autumn in 1349, Agrigör, it is said, has need of but two seasons: Winter and *Deep* Winter. I was alone, save my inebriated guidesman, who asked only to be paid in Horrand mead. A hasty sort, he naturally demanded his payment up front, and while he did indeed locate the trail, he found it so narrow that his befuddled gait was insufficient, and as I checked his makeshift map to ensure we were making proper progress, I turned back to find he had vanished.

By the time I recognized his contriturated form, liquefied on the boulders far below the steppe, what had been a light snowfall soon graduated into a squall of considerable power. In short order, the path, which could previously be distinguished only by a dark brown foot trail, disappeared beneath sheets of blinding white, and almost at once I found I was without bearing, my map rendered useless (and the parchment it was scrawled upon water damaged by the snows to boot). Only the vague winding direction against the steep mountain lent the faintest clue to my destination, so I dispensed with some of my less useful belongings—I ruefully report that my leather-bound Mandius' Almanac yr. 920 Ed. was a casualty of this decision—and charted a more vertical course, foothold by foothold, crag by weather-beaten crag. My advance was slow, but deliberate, yet even bundled as I was in the finest furs, I soon found my breathing strained and extremities numbed by the brutal elements.

It was such that when my hand fumbled for a grip and found instead a strange smooth surface during my climb, midway up the mountain, I thus believed frostbite had finally claimed all feeling in my fingers. Further inspection, however, revealed strange symbols carven upon its surface, highlighted by feathery snow. Fortunately, I retained the presence of mind and the strength of body to scrawl them in charcoal upon a strip of leather, from which they are hereby presented:

$$\varphi \; \oplus \; \partial \; 1 \; (\; \smile$$

As bizarre an occurrence as it was, it might have been written off as the accidental discovery of a Karnish mining tunnel or perhaps the remnants of an Agrigör precursor settlement. What settled it was the figure that soon emerged from the blizzard, standing almost upright, on a more lateral stretch of the mountainside. At first, only its outline was dimly visible, but I could discern already that it stood no larger than a young child, 3, perhaps 4, heads. Buried in the snow, trudging with purpose, seemed to be two legs clad in oversized boots. This persuaded me at first that I had located some Horrand youth, as I am aware of their custom to keep their progeny clad in the same oversized attire for years on end until they might still don it full grown. Then came a break in the wall of sleet, which disabused me of this notion entirely.

What I found myself looking upon, at first, seemed some manner of large animal that had been cruelly dressed in Valen garb or something approximating it. The ornamentation remained utterly foreign to me. A tunic of dull blue fell to what must have been the creature's knees, which donned child-sized breeches of some dark color (brown, perhaps?) and a fur overcloak with a fine brocade hood obscuring its facial features. At the end of each arm seemed to be large mitts, and at first I assumed it wore some manner of oversized glove, for there were five sharp and clawed digits protruded from the bulky appendages, and we have heard tell of similar gloved and bladed weapons worn by Bord assassins. Yet this creature was several sizes smaller even than the diminutive reptile folk of Nazgan. As it neared—unaware, at first, of my presence, for I was by then all but buried in a layer of snow and must have looked like a rock formation—I saw these were no gloves, but what passed for the thing's hands. It must have spotted me with surprise, for it paused in place. At once, a gust of fell wind struck us both, and its features stood revealed.

The only word I can find to describe it is "mole." The features were a somewhat more expressive and mannish variant of a common garden-variety mole. Black-brown wiry fur coated its entire head, save a bare snout which extended some distance between two beady, but sympathetic eyes and a small nose, reddening in the wintry gale, protruding from the end of it.

I was of course aware of the persistent folk tales of the Delvers. Pseudo-scholars even purported to know their chosen name—Gorrum—for the past several centuries. All were discredited nearly as quickly.

I am here to report that they were repudiated in error. The Delvers *do* exist. In short order, I was informed by the creature—in the most densely accented Talorn speech I have ever heard—that the smooth surface I had chanced upon was a passage. He seemed frightened and leery, and he bade me allow him to pass. Being in no state to refuse him, even if I'd wished, I acceded. Which is to say, I remained prone and did not move, all strength having abandoned me.

It was then that I passed from consciousness and remembered nothing until I emerged from near delirium in a Blackcroft healing hall three days subsequent, my fever having only recently broken. The stranger, apparently, had managed to deposit me on the doorstep of the establishment, with gemstones in my knapsack sufficient for payment. (One must marvel at the apparent strength of a being of such slight stature.)

Dismiss these as the fevered ravings of a hypothermic lunatic at your peril. What I can recall from our discourse makes plain an entire civilization of these Delvers dots the entire continent of Trávinás, dwarfing any other power by sheer surface area alone. One phrase I recall distinctly. "Passage to Mordas." If it sounds familiar, the reason is that many of the folk tales concerning such Delvers have recurrently mentioned this word. Is Mordas a resource? A place? A kingdom? Perhaps even a race or subset of these Delver folk?

Sadly, my present infirmity forbids a return trip to relocate this Mordas Passage. But I recount without hesitation: This door exists, and with some effort, might yet be found, on the outskirts of Blackcroft, high in the Agrigör Mountains. Upon, and behind it, lay secrets generations of Valen scholars have speculated upon and even denounced.

With the proper funding and a miraculous recovery, I intend to prove these lesser minds wrong."

—Excerpt from "Tarrying To and Fro"
By Tarius Varon
1357

This humble recorder presents this excerpt with neither derision nor endorsement and in faith that future generations will discern the fact or fiction of it.

Section II
The Valen Calendar

Though the Aviári are believed to have been the first to establish a formal calendar and to mark the passage of time numerically (even if recent evidence suggests Men, Bords, and even Horrands employed similar, if non-standardized and non-written, systems prior to recorded time) it was the Valen calendar which all nations, save Highcrest, employ today. It is, of course, derived from an earlier version of the Aviári calendar and, as such, features words and allusions to figures of Aven myth.

The similarities are obvious when one compares a standard Aven week:

Nárlánár
Wyváilánár
Ráilánár
Hûelánár
Átrilánár
Setrálánár
Ánálánár

...to the seven days of a standard Valen week, which progress as follows:

Ashday
Lorday
Vicday
Trisday
Creaday
Fallday
Maiday

To drive the similarities home: Ráilánár, which is known in Vale as VicDay, translates from Aven speech as Victory Day. While even more obviously, Setrálánár, which falls on the same day of the week as Fallday, translates literally as Fallday in the Aven language.

The full Valen calendar for the year of this volume's publication is as follows:

Yr. 1851

Ántilián

Ash	Lor	Vic	Tris	Crea	Fall	Mai
				1	2	3
4	5	6	7	8	9	10
11	12	13	14	15	16	17
18	19	20	21	22	23	24
25	26	27	28	29	30	31

Vilnás

A	L	V	T	C	F	M
1	2	3	4	5	6	7
8	9	10	11	12	13	14
15	16	17	18	19	20	21
22	23	24	25	26	27	28

APPENDIX

Dögn

A	L	V	T	C	F	M
1	2	3	4	5	6	7
8	9	10	11	12	13	14
15	16	17	18	19	20	21
22	23	24	25	26	27	28
29	30	31				

Leviás

A	L	V	T	C	F	M
			1	2	3	4
5	6	7	8	9	10	11
12	13	14	15	16	17	18
19	20	21	22	23	24	25
26	27	28	29	30		

Torgan

A	L	V	T	C	F	M
					1	2
3	4	5	6	7	8	9
10	11	12	13	14	15	16
17	18	19	20	21	22	23
24	25	26	27	28	29	30
31						

Drognos

A	L	V	T	C	F	M
	1	2	3	4	5	6
7	8	9	10	11	12	13
14	15	16	17	18	19	20
21	22	23	24	25	26	27
28	29	30				

DEATH MASK

Valárist

A	L	V	T	C	F	M
			1	2	3	4
5	6	7	8	9	10	11
12	13	14	15	16	17	18
19	20	21	22	23	24	25
26	27	28	29	30	31	

Cáthmir

A	L	V	T	C	F	M
						1
2	3	4	5	6	7	8
9	10	11	12	13	14	15
16	17	18	19	20	21	22
23	24	25	26	27	28	29
30	31					

Kemliá

A	L	V	T	C	F	M
		1	2	3	4	5
6	7	8	9	10	11	12
13	14	15	16	17	18	19
20	21	22	23	24	25	26
27	28	29	30			

Ánái

A	L	V	T	C	F	M
				1	2	3
4	5	6	7	8	9	10
11	12	13	14	15	16	17
18	19	20	21	22	23	24
25	26	27	28	29	30	31

Vidris

A	L	V	T	C	F	M
1	2	3	4	5	6	7
8	9	10	11	12	13	14
15	16	17	18	19	20	21
22	23	24	25	26	27	28
29	30					

Sórn

A	L	V	T	C	F	M
		1	2	3	4	5
6	7	8	9	10	11	12
13	14	15	16	17	18	19
20	21	22	23	24	25	26
27	28	29	30	31		

Trávinás: An Abridged History

What follows being a truncated account of
Westerland history as far back as such was recorded

There have been many methods used to demarcate specific periods in our great continent's history. Even somewhat pedestrian means of simply numbering each individual time period and recording it as a "First Age" or "Second Age." Thankfully, due to the adoption of the Aven calendar across the continent, these crude instruments have since been abandoned for more illustrative and evocative methods of describing our events and times. While Trávinás does indeed have "eras," anyone of sufficient academic comprehension is better served titling them after the events that predominated during said period. What follows is a cursory summary, at best, and many periods of prolonged peace, events not recorded in a Valen hand, or those involving matters sensitive to the security of the state are unrecorded herein.

The Nascent Years

"Breath of Ánái,
Wind of creation,
Favor of Lyntia,
Womb of the World,
Fire of Sorn,
Crucible of conception,
Night of Adon,
Dawn of dissolution."

—Canticles of Faricott, *Oracle of Ánái*, 215–271

No reliable reckoning has yet been forwarded for the Nascent Years. "Creation" is delineated in many myths, some with verifiable claim in terms of names, places, or known grave sites... others believed metaphorical or spiritual.

While each culture has its apportioned explanation and philosophy, many taking on religious significance, this Recorder feels it untoward to impose our own within these pages. Long years were the Driváni worshiped. Longer have they reputedly slumbered in the distant continent far to the East. But this is the accepted belief in Vale, as originated from the ancient Aviári, and while elements of it can be found in many of the cultures across the continent, nearly as many differ in virtually every respect.

What is mutual in all stories is that, together or apart, nearly all races of Trávinás began in Highcrest with the Aviári being among the first to chisel their fortresses from mountain rock while Men migrated south into Vale and the Bords took residence in the swamps south of Alcaire before their dubious reputation bade them relocate farther still into the desert peaks and high wastelands of Nazgan. Nestled beneath the Aven peoples, in the Aven Valleys and the Forest of Alcaire, lay the tribal Ferássûn, a pastoral, wolven people, who spent much of their early history avoiding the affairs of Men and the Aviári. It is said they were different in appearance at that time. they were less human and more wolflike, and some sources allege it was their gradually increasing association with the Aven peoples that made them moreso like Men.

144

APPENDIX

The Horrands are a matter of some debate. A plurality of Horrands today believe they spawned alongside the others while many contemporaneous accounts theorize the Horrands were once Men who migrated south into the snows and were hardened and adapted to the elements. A recent school of thought holds that the Horrands were descended from beasts and became more manlike in aspect as they civilized. This, they argue, accounts for their radical physical transformation once possessed by the Vehemence, the Valen name for the transmogrifying bloodrage which few Horrands survive.

Of the Delvers, if we even accept their existence as rote... little is written. For, if they do walk our lands, their primary traffic with the Uplanders (their rumored name for Valen folk) consists of trade and mercantile, and the mysteries of their origins, civilization, and language remain obfuscatory.

The Aven people advanced the fastest and became the first to establish a common calendar and names for each month and day of the week. The Aven Empire continues to iterate on this calendar while Valen society still employs this earlier variant with some more modern modifications of its own. It was at this point that the recording of time was undertaken by the earliest Aviári recorders, and their painstaking notes (though often lost) comprise a surprisingly complete record of the latter years of the Nascent Era.

Dawnlight Empire

Yr. 1–570 (Est.)

> *"The Dawnlight Empire was not a great civilization.*
> *The Dawnlight Empire **created** civilization."*

> —Ónigón, *Lyntári Eve 871 Address*,
> Emperor of Highcrest, 864–924

The Golden Age of the Aven Empire, first to establish an ordered, law-given civilization and to construct sprawling, walled cities united by a single spiritual vision. A vision which was spread through a vast empire, which soon spanned two-thirds of the continent. The other nations of Vale, Göurnoth, and Nazgan slowly followed suit, but for over half a millennium, the Aviári boasted both the first and the loftiest empire ever constructed.

Aven Decline

571–899

> *"The measure of a man is not in how he navigates his ascent,*
> *but in how he weathers the inevitable plummet."*

> —Punerius Hastercroft, *Xanthum: A Tragedy*,
> Novelist and Playwright, 1302–1351

Domestic adversity, infighting between the three Aven imperial bloodlines, and a revolt at the hands of their slave-class, the Ferás-sûn, saw the Aven Empire fall from prominence to anomie. Worse still, as rumblings emerged of a sect of Valen Men who had mastered the arcane to an equal or greater degree as the colleges of Lyndenál, the Aven claim over the chaotic force of magicka was soon challenged. The group, which came to be called the Beholden, would ultimately dismantle the Aviári's previous stranglehold over the arts. Though, as history would show, they would guard the same secrets even more jealously than had their winged contemporaries.

As the Empire of the Wing collapsed, their efforts to secularize and provide for the public welfare stunted the empire's growth. The Kingdom of Vale benefited most from the disunion.

The Sanguine Century

900–999

> *"Every race of the continent was drawn into the strife. Each suffered. Each*
> *bled. And victory was purchased with countless lives from each."*

APPENDIX

—*"The War of the Rift"* by Galion Kallevus,
Recorder, Tirionus, 12th Ántilián, 1411

The War of the Rift (929–985) remains the deadliest conflict in the history of the explored world. A nameless force, marching under no banner and making no political or territorial demands erupted from the Rift (the vast, unexplained chasm spanning the entirety of the northern continental border—whose origin is credited, or blamed, to the Aviári's ancient experimentation with the forces of magick and chaos) in the north, they fell upon the Aven Empire, which was only beginning to rebuild. Before its bloody conclusion, every nation in the Westerlands would involve itself in the War of the Rift, recognizing that this Darkling Horde (as it came to be called) was insurmountable by any single military force. Though the enemy withdrew after a final stand in the Aven Valleys, the scars of this apocalyptic conflict remain upon the land and the diplomatic dynamics of every major power in the Westerlands.

The aftermath, with its hushed whispers of a rogue mage of the Beholden, whose forbidden ambitions may have conjured or provoked whatever this Darkling Horde might have been, served only as a prelude to a greater conflict, when matters of wider political intrigue intervened.

The 10th century only became truly Sanguine when its sequel, "the Horrand/Ferás-sûn War," (986–991) consumed Göurnoth and High-crest. The Sanguine Century left all nations save Vale utterly ravaged.

The Menuvian Era

1000–1110

> *"Our Lady [Anaris] delivered more men from thralldom from the comfort of her bedchambers than any Menuvian pikeman at the front lines of Aphelan. And while wielding deadlier weapons."*

—*"The State of The State"* by *"X"*, 1078

The Golden Age of the Menuvian Crown. With the Aviári and Bords caught in successor politics and still rebuilding from the War of the Rift, and the Horrands and Ferás-sûn devastated by their half-decade military conflagration, the stage was set for the ascent of Men. The Kingdom of Vale prospered under the rule of Thumus (997–1050) and the first Queen, Lady Anaris, "the Ethereal Lady," (1050–1097) though as their Aven neighbors to the north began to settle affairs, they also began to interfere in Valen court politics more and more. The Aven Spy Scandal (1090) made clear the Aviári viewed Men as a threat and were working to bring about their downfall.

Dominion of the Wing

1110–1173

𝕽𝕬𝕽ⓔ𝕱𝕵𝕰𝕵𝕽𝕽𝕺𝕴𝕵𝕽ⓔ𝕺𝕵𝕮𝕲𝕽𝕱𝕵𝕷𝕲 .

"*Aviári wái ráiás kó fáián lir dilás wái sylá.*"
"*Aven ambition dies slowly, and with malice.*"

—Ánáis, (yr. 209)

An act of Menuvian retribution for the Aven Spy Scandal of 1090 gave the Aviári pretext to counterattack. In truth, it was no reprisal, the Aven military forces having been camped along the Vale/Highcrest/Nazgani border for a period of 5 years, preparing to spring just this snare. Vale was caught completely off guard and was overwhelmed by the massive army bivouacked at their border. Compounding the calamity, the Aven emperor struck a deal with the Karnish city of Sensenal—to the south-east, within Vale's borders—to supply them for the assault. Menuvian soldiers were being cut down by swords forged within their own borders. This led to the majority of the Valen nation living under occupation by the Dominion of the Wing (1110–1173) with an open resistance persisting in the south. Lady Anaris II (1139–1171) met with Aven Emperor Leváras (1138–1200) to strike a deal. The occupation became a vassal's alliance, as the emperor was utterly taken by the Queen's half-Aven beauty and proposed marriage. Anaris II, however, hatched the Wedding Coup on the day they were to consummate. She hired half the

Aven guard to behead their commanders while quietly promising vast concessions to their allies in Sensenal to march on the cathedral on the day of the wedding.

Anaris II had won her kingdom back in a bloody, heartless coup. Emperor Levárás, who was allowed to flee, still loved her until his dying day.

The Cerulean Empire

1173–1204

> *"To soar with the winged ones or be swatted as flies.*
> *The hour of our Empire affords no alternative."*

—Ashran, Usurper King (1171–1204)

In order to secure the Wedding Coup, Anaris II was forced to agree to Menuvia's military being incorporated into Sensenal's. The First General of Sensenal was a Karnish military genius and swordsman named Ashran (1171–1204). The general warmed to the young queen and she to him. Until the day she was suddenly assassinated.

Ashran produced a document, in the queen's own hand, giving the Sensenal First General (himself) emergency powers in the event of her death as a result of aggression. Ashran was installed as interim ruler, and after a series of purges of the Menuvian nobility (and the installation of his own New Patrician class, loyal to him) within one year, he was vested as Emperor of Menuvia. (The title of king was denied him, for his blood was neither royal nor noble.)

He spoke passionately of an "empire that spans to the Cerulean Gulf," implying the need to strike back at the Dominion of the Wing, which still occupied much of northern Vale. Over years of bloody conflict, this Cerulean Empire (1173–1204) stretched across Vale, occupied half of Göurnoth, colonized Nazgan, and flushed the Aven occupiers out of Arkwood. Emperor Levárás himself dueled Ashran amid the ruins of the Aven temple of Kemliá (today the ruin of Dirás-Viórûs). He was no match for the swordcraft of Menuvia's Usurper and lost an arm in their combat, dying a few years later, having failed to avenge his former lover. The Cerulean Empire then drove into Highcrest to complete its revenge. It was there Ashran made his fatal error: a simultaneous strike—dividing his armies in two—on Highcrest city itself and the Aven capital of Válieri. On his way, Ashran put the orchards of Kathylón (the Ferás-sûn capital) to the torch to prevent their interference. By the time they assaulted the Aviári, they found the Ferás-sûn had joined with their former slavemasters as allies of convenience in order to gain their own revenge.

The Cerulean Empire was defeated at Highcrest and fought to a fruitless stalemate at Válieri. Ashran ordered a full retreat and took his top general's head.

He would be assassinated before he could rebuild and respond. A robed figure would unleash unbridled chaos from his fist, destroying the entire general staff, himself, Ashran, and most of the Menuvian Citadel in the process. The Cerulean Empire had fallen.

Union of the Twin Kingdoms

1253–1291

> "The blades of Tirionus and Sensenal crossed for the final time when they were woven upon our standard. Never again shall they meet, so long as I live."

—Caedran II, King of Tirionus (1723–1772)

After a year of murderous civil strife, the Menuvian royal line was reinstalled. Recognizing Menuvian nobility, and the throne, had been compromised, King Tirion (1253–1270), known as Trivnius, would have the capital city moved from Menuvia to the larger city of Calmon, just to the north. It was renamed Tirionus, after himself, and new currency was printed bearing his name as well. Yet for all this seeming vanity, his next move would be to divide his power. Recognizing the ambition of his southwestern neighbors in Sensenal and how it had nearly brought Vale to ruin, Tirion became the first Valen king to recognize the legitimacy of the Karnish crown. He signed the Tirion-Doreth Pact (on Ántilián 12th, 1254) and established the first dual monarchy in Valen history.

Sensenal would provide the military and industry base while Tirionus would be the political and mercantile center of the empire. After the assassination of Tirion (the third in a row) by a conspiracy of incensed Menuvian nobility (read: *The Order of the Ebon Flame: From Nobles to Assassins*, Ulian Darwick [1781]) the Twin Monarchy afforded the nation surprisingly stability with Doreth acting in his fallen comrade's stead. To ease the tensions in the supplanted Menuvia, the city was afforded its very own Senate to give it at least the appearance of a voice in national affairs.

The Horrand Menace

1291–1293

> *"Horrand blood is a fine fuel for war but a poor sustenance for rulership."*

> —Ovyron the Seer, Mage (1842)

Taking advantage of the dramas of succession on their northern border, the Horrands launched several successful assaults on Vale as vengeance for the territory lost during the Cerulean Empire. Yet they were more successful conquerors than colonists, and their reign lasted fewer than 3 years before they were driven out by a well-organized resistance force known as the Knights of the Rapier.

Thereafter, the knights were installed as the official Elite Guard of Tirionus, an order which persists to this day.

The Age of the Hammer

1294–1450

> *"To the Horrands, what is theirs.*
> *To the Birds, whatever they can keep."*

DEATH MASK

—Firth Thirk, (1408–1443)

Conquering Vale had not been Göurnoth's true plan, but a simple contingency to ease its true aim: the conquest of Highcrest and vengeance for Aviári treachery during the Cerulean Empire's reign. Making rapid technological advancements which were kept behind an iron wall of secrecy, Göurnoth had quietly constructed the largest naval fleet ever seen. They dispatched a massive expeditionary force which conquered and occupied much of the western half of Highcrest, including the imperial seat of Válieri (which was renamed Nargoth (Hammerthrone in the language of Agrigör, a show of defiance after the language was outlawed following the failed occupation of Vale). This colony of New Göurnoth would subsist for over a century, culminating in the Firth of Göurnoth himself, Gäfönoth (1334–1369), relocating to the captured Aven capital to occupy the throne.

Known as "the Age of the Hammer" among the Horrands and Men, and "the Century of Sleet" by the Aviári. For, in order to dislodge the occupiers, the now-secularized Aven Empire uncharacteristically turned to its arcane past. The Lyndenáli Archmage summoned occult power, which—as ever—proved a faithless art. The chaotic summoning achieved the opposite of its intended effect: an unceasing, supernatural blizzard, which drove off the Aviári from the newly inhospitable landscape, leaving the Horrands of New Göurnoth entrenched.

It was only after a new Aven Empress (Lady Váriá, 1406–1458) commissioned the disgraced mages of Lyndenál to utilize a final desperate spell that they successfully summoned a sea of fire from the snow-swept mountains of Highcrest to wash the enemies of the Aviári away in a sea of molten rock, that the age was ended in 1450. The origin of the fire of deliverance remains a subject of debate. For the mountains were undamaged in the effort and did not appear volcanic.

Twin facts which suggest that it may have been summoned from the Rift itself.

The Age of Endeavor

1450–1690

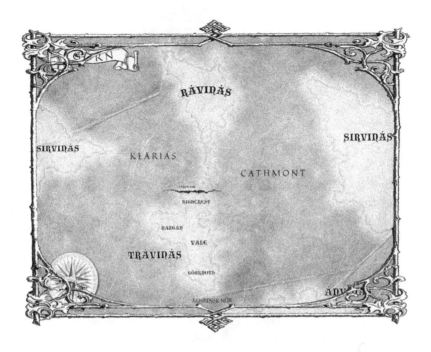

"Horizon beckons yonder,
Ambition burns abreast,
Tis the feeble soul that wanders,
Bold hearts yield conquest."

—Dänar Kolyss, Horrand Explorer and Bard (1393)

Following the resolution of the Horrand/Aviári conflicts, the empires of Trávinás began to stabilize. With a Loreális Empress on the Aven throne, trade to the south was opened, and Göurnoth, under new Firth Öron IV (1472–1505) exchanged naval secrets to acquire valuable resources needed to rebuild his shattered armies. In Vale, the Union of the Twin Kingdoms unshackled its industry, and the combination of this new technology and an ascendant merchant caste led to the establishment of a sizable fleet, formally commissioned jointly by King Kerryn of Tirionus and Queen Alasirus of Sensenal in 1515.

In the innumerable expeditions to follow, the northern continent of Rávinás, only cursorily charted by aerial scouts from Highcrest previously, was roughly mapped in 1535, though attempts to land were forestalled by the treacherous currents caused by the Rift which spans the southern tip of the continent, until 1553, when Milius Tealcroft set anchor off the shores of the continent.

Though he never returned, subsequent exhibitions did locate the remains of his vessel, with a partially burned log which spoke of a reptilian, horned, hostile race, larger and more austere than the Bords, who trafficked in a strange tongue.

Two other land masses—Ánvinás and Sirvinás—were spotted, though only the former was explored, and at least to the present, appears uninhabited, even by wildlife. The borders of Sirvinás were a matter of worldwide interest, for religious orders and scholars of myth still retell the tales of the Driváni believed to be slumbering in the Easterlands far across the vast Sea of Cathmont.

Sirvinás, sadly, appears beyond the abilities of most naval vessels to reliably reach, and only one exhausted aerial scout of Highcrest has yet spotted it, perishing before she could fully recount the tale. In the latter part of this Age of Endeavor, as Emperor Lásádár [1509–1558] famously named it in an imperial address, the discovery of iron ore in Nazgan led to an industrial boom in the 17th century, from which Vale benefited the most, yet all nations of the Westerlands would benefit from the leap forward in technological prowess during this period.

The Breaking of The Beholden

1700–1799

"Nothing cultivates so much speculation, misjudgement or animus as a mystery.
Nothing, save its answer."

—Morwyte the Discerning, Elder of The Beholden
(Rumored) 1794

The years of peace and prosperity were broken when a raid on a Lyndenáli crimelord's mansion revealed the archmages had not summoned the sea of fire to end the Age of the Hammer by themselves but had instead contracted the Beholden to do the deed for them. A matter of major controversy, for the Beholden were and are a secretive and ancient order, as much occult historians as the only official mage's guild of Trávinás. The Beholden were now blamed for the Age of the Hammer and the Horrand/Ferás-sûn War, but the documents also suggested they had been summoning and experimenting with fell magic from the Rift for centuries beyond count. this was a risible accusation, not merely because of the clandestine nature of the Beholden but also due to the long and documented history of magic as an uncontrollable, chaotic force.

Beyond their meddlings in the many wars of Westerlands—and near-irreparable damage to the climate of Highcrest—the Beholden were alleged to have been responsible for upheavals and heresies stretching back long before magick was even a known and acknowledged quantity.

Among the more recent imputations: In 1204, the Usurper Ashran was assassinated in what could only be described as a complete eruption of chaotic force. ("Musings of a Disgraced Vizier" [1221]) While few mourned the tyrant's immolation, fewer were comforted by the prospect of mage assassins vaporizing their leaders with a snap of their fingers. Beholden involvement was widely believed, but never established ir-refutably. Menuvian sentiment has ever run against magick, but it has risen to a roar ever since.

In 1290, what witnesses could only describe as a Wave of Flame spanned much of the southwestern Valen countryside at the height of hostilities between the Horrands and Men. Whatever fell power ani-mated the phenomenon made the land thereafter barren to the point of being nigh-uninhabitable. It was just so that it came by the ominous eponym of "the Plains of the Unclean," doubly so for the common legal practice of banishing criminals, prostitutes and other plague carriers to their desolate tracts. That most Horrands had evacuated the plains before the phenomenon consumed fully one-fourth of the Valen Imperial Military still leads many to suspect it was unleashed, under contract, by Beholden mages for hire. A practice explicitly forbidden by their creed under penalty of expulsion or death. These were just two examples of dozens in which the Beholden, or their rogue apostles, were believed to have either escalated or interfered in global intrigue at the cost of human lives. For a coven of impassive observers whose stated mission is to record human history objectively while safeguarding its most dangerous secrets... it was clear to many, particularly in the Valen Senate, that the overseers had become something more active and potentially sinister.

Whatever the truth, by 1701, mass demonstrations against the order emerged in most major cities of the Westerlands, and they were being formally blamed for summoning the Darkling Horde which had incited the War of the Rift. (This is an accusation we still do not know the veracity of.)

Pogroms and open violence followed, and the Beholden were forced to enlist their own protective force, which the other nations interpreted as a private army. The real or perceived sufferings of the Beholden—and their leadership's insistence on remaining impassive, non-violent, and detached—led to a schism in which a group known as the Open Eye began to conspire and retaliate in defense of their art. In time, these defensive acts became more outwardly aggressive. When the Open Eye attempted to hem in a marching Horrand army intent on razing a mage's apothecary in Uplith, their spell to summon hail instead split the earth, resulting in a dozen lives lost and an entire city block split in two. The Open Eye was primarily comprised of inexperienced acolytes, whose expertise was unequal to their masters.

The people of Trávinás—spurred by a newly emerging journalist class—took this as certain proof that the Beholden may have unwittingly created the Rift itself in years long past. Uncertain of the claims' credulity but unable to quell the disquiet, the great powers of the Westerlands were forced to confer for the Conference of Aphelan (1791). It was decided the Beholden must disband and the Open Eye be imprisoned (or executed, as the Horrands prescribed, though a mage operating in the anti-magic south would be a reckless fool indeed).

As it turned out, Göurnoth had been their hiding place all along. The ancient summoning grounds high in mountains southwest of DarkForge known as the Auguras Crag.

The Open Eye made a last stand at the crag, aware they were unequal to the multinational force that surrounded them. They were vanquished in near totality.

The remaining Beholden agreed to disband, forbidden to practice arcane craft under penalty of death.

Upheavals of Nazgan and The Age of Great Prosperity

1800—Present

> *"Peace, too, is a form of war. Entailing at least as much intrigue, strategy, and subterfuge as any conflict to ever ravage our continent. It is a war I intend to win."*

—King Draylon of Sensenal (Royal Address, 1849)

What has followed since the breaking of the Beholden is a period of peace to rival the Age of Endeavor. The Twin Kingdoms have provided stability and progress, interrupted only briefly by the usurpations of the Bords of Nazgan, who dispossessed the empire of its long-held Karathis outpost in 1817. While the blow to the economy was initially apprised as great, renewed ties with our Horrand allies in the south have more than made up the difference in ore and other natural resources. Nazgan, ever an epicentre of intrigue, suffered its own internal usurpations, as the Cataclysm of 1850, and the subsequent purge of the remaining L'Intáza nobles readily attests. Perhaps most disquieting is the allegation, by some among the Zi'Zin Temple, that the Cataclysm (a tremendous quaking of the earth and wall of water that swept clean nearly half the country) was unnatural in origin. Leaving an open question whether the Beholden ever truly disbanded, or if one of their disgraced order kept an unnamed apprentice. Perhaps, some suggest, even many.

Kings Relegant and Draylon sit on the thrones of Tirionus and Sensenal, respectably, and are fast friends from the latter's youth to the former's elder days. Vinris rules the Aven throne, his kingdom utterly committed now to the isolationist philosophies of "Vinvánás wái Tyvás" (the Aven philosophy formalized in the pages of the Twinfall Accords [989], which stipulated the primacy of domestic affairs over international intrigue and trade). Their Ferás-sûn neighbors have again splintered, not out of disunity, but in a welcome age of expansion and exploration. Once all but invisible outside of Highcrest's borders, today the presence of a Wolven citizen roaming the Valen woods or even working in the silver mines of Nazgan is not so rare a sight. The Horrands are again fractious, but less warlike, under the even-tempered Firth Grädör of DarkForge, and after Vale's initial aggression in Nazgan had passed, Sálár Shi'Átás has sidestepped numerous scandals to become a credible and cunning queen, formally recognized by Vale and other nations.

This humble Recorder can only hope the threats of Republican upheaval in Menuvia, the peasant revolts in Romatho, and the strange rumors out of Sensenal are simply that: rumor.

—Jerith Marcand
Recorder, Tirionus
18th Dögn, 1851

Lexicon of Trávinás

What follows being a list of common terms, names and places and their associated definitions to the people of the Westerlands

Ádón: "Lord of the Night." Driváni of darkness and disrepute. Rival of Ánái for the affections of Lady Lyntiá and her creations. Varying myths stipulate his fate: From execution to conversion to perpetual imprisonment in a nameless cave in Göurnoth.

Áfá: Foremost criminal cartel in Nazgan. As thievery and assassination is legal in Kara'Zin, it is also regulated heavily. The Áfá serve both as commissioners and regulators of all larcenous activity in Nazgan, and also a valued branch of its government.

Agrigör: Northern region of Göurnoth, typified by sweeping tundras in the center and south, and snow-capped peaks in the north. Its largest, walled city, "Agrigör," was once the capital of Göurnoth and seat of the Firth from 309–999. Many Horrands who oppose the DarkForge Firth still consider it to be the rightful seat of the throne. "Agrigör" can also refer to the near-dead tongue spoken by the Horrand people. (see: Agrigörian)

158

APPENDIX

Age of Endeavor: Period from 1450–1690, marked by advancements in naval craft, technology and even the pursuit of the arcane arts.

Agrigörian: (or "Agrigör") The guttural and ancient tongue of the Horrand folk. Unofficially outlawed after the Age of the Hammer, it continues to be spoken in the snowy south.

Akhrensk-Nûr: Icy seas that span the gap between the southern tip of Göurnoth and the mysterious continent of Ánvinás.

A'lidar Desert: Largest desert in Trávinás, accounting for the overwhelming surface area of the nation of Nazgan.

Ánái: Foremost of the Driváni, and lord of light and warmth.

Ántólás: Rebel slave, expert warrior and folk hero of the Ferás-sûn. His rebellion against his Aven slavemasters, achieving their complete liberation by 730.

Ánvinás: Southernmost continent of Górn. It has been tentatively explored and found to be uninhabited, even by any visible wildlife. (see: Age of Endeavor)

Aphelan: Fishing village along the northeast Cerulean Coast of Vale, at the far edge of Arkwood Forest.

Aven: (See: Aviári)

Aviári: "People of the Wing." The winged people of Northern Highcrest, an ancient civilization organized around occupational castes, rather than region or ancestry. (Alternate: "Aven")

Bal-Ashid, Domus: (1839–present) Prominent, charismatic senator who arose from humble beginnings to become the exemplar of Menuvia's ascendant political class. A strong advocate for the establishment of a Valen Republic, (See: Menuvian Republic Movement) though he claims this needn't necessarily end in the termination of the Twin Kingdom.

Beholden: Guardians of the ancient arts for centuries, and silent recorders of history and knowledge. With the Breaking of the Beholden (1700–1799) their order has splintered. Though the arcane arts will ever attract the curious or ambitious.

Blackcroft: Mountainous smithy village high in the Agrigör Mountains, seated at the border of Vale and Göurnoth. Its population is a contentious mix of Man and Horrand.

Bord: The squat, reptilian peoples who migrated from the southwestern marshes of Highcrest to Nazgan some time during the Nascent Years. Long believed nomads, the Bords have since settled Kara'Zin as their "reclaimed capital".

Calmon: Grand, walled city which was razed during the Cerulean Empire (1173–1204). Rebuilt, it now serves as the site of Tirionus, one of the Twin Capitals of Vale.

Cerulean Empire: The regime of the "Cerulean Usurper," Lord Ashran, which first focused on throwing the Domninion of the Wing out of Vale, and then on conquest of Highcrest itself. Ended with the assassination of the despot in 1204.

Cerulean Gulf: Body of water which touches the southeastern borders of Highcrest and the northeastern border of Vale. One of the most valuable trading port of Trávinás.

Cröd: A massive, herbivorous beast native to Göurnoth and southern Vale. Harmless until confronted, they are hunted for sport and sunstenance, particularly by the Horrands and Kiá.

DarkForge: Capital of Göurnoth. Seat of power for the Horrand Firths.

Darklings: The word given the mysterious, ash-skinned race that emerged from The Rift in 929, marking the commencement of The War of the Rift. Their name derives from the black banner under which they marked, representing no nation known in the Westerlands.

APPENDIX

Delvers: (See: Gorrim)

Draylon: King of Sensenal (1822–present) a longer-serving King than his friend Relegant, but a much younger man.

Driváni: ("Divine Ones.") Mythic lords believed responsible for all of creation, each race the favored child of each. After doing battle with Adon, myths differ on what next transpired, but all end with the Driváni either dying, or hibernating in the East.

Emperor of Highcrest: Sovereign ruler of the Aven people. Representing an unbroken line from Válieri (136–209) to Vinris (1840–present).

Felroth, Gregus: "Peasant King." Former senator, Tirionus noble and philanthropist. A childhood friend of King Relegant, he has attempted to mediate the dispute between the White Banner peasants and their King.

Ferás-sûn: The "Wolven" peoples of Southern Highcrest, residing primarily in the forest of Alcaire or the riverbanks of Highcrest. The Ferás-sûn comprised the slave class of Aven society until the Ántólás insurrection. (see: Ántólás)

Firth: Lord of Göurnoth. Frequently challenged and even broken, the current line of DarkForge Firths nevertheless persists, with Grädor (1824–present). A perpetual conflict between rival Horrand Houses (See: Thörg)—and the Kräga in their employ— inevitably results in a single sovereign "Firth," whose seat lies at the heart of the city of DarkForge and (theoretically) rules above all others.

Ghostwind: Environmental phenomenon observed in the A'lidar desert of Nazgan. Particularly intense in the portion of land known colloquially as the Whispering Waste.

Gör: Herbivorous beasts of burden with massive legs and thick hides, as prized for war as transport. Native to Nazgan and Western Vale.

Gorrim: ("Delvers.") The squat and molelike race rumored for centuries to dwell in vast "underkingdoms" beneath all four nations of Trávinás. The grandest of these is reputed to be called "Mordas".

Górn: The World, as named by the Aviári. Covered predominately with water and the land masses of Trávinás, Sirvinás, Ánvinás and Rávinás.

Göurnoth: Southernmost nation of Trávinás, populated by the stalwart Horrand people. A frigid landscape of frozen plains and rugged mountain ranges. It borders Vale in the north. Its southern coast is spanned by the sea of Akhrensk-Nûr and to the east by the Sea of Cathmont.

Gromir: (Rumored) Language of the "Gorrim" people. (See: Delvers)

Gûntaug: (See: Ghostwind)

Highcrest: Verdant and craggy country to the north of Vale where the Aviári and Ferás-sûn reside. Its southwestern border spans the tip of Nazgan, and its eastern coast comprises the Sea of Cathmont and Cerulean Gulf, while the west coast borders the Kariás Ocean. Its entire northern border is subsumed by the bizarre expanse its people call Lithióláin (see: The Rift).

Horrand: The hardy mountain folk of Göurnoth. A clannish and fractious society that vacillates between united allegiance to a warlord called a "Firth," and a collection of sovereign houses that employ a warrior class to vanquish their rivals.

Ín: (Izákás) Bordish word for "Fortress" or "Citadel".

Izákas: Language of The Bords, and one of their most closely-held secrets for many centuries.

Jägen: "Constancy." One of the virtues of the Kräga warrior class in Göurnoth.

Jáhár: (Izákás) Bordish word, meaning "breeze" or more illustratively, "windy gale".

APPENDIX

Jeh'Mhár: Bordish nobles, whose K'rás Council serves as a branch of Nazgani government.

Kariás: (Keärias) Vast and treacherous ocean that spans the western coast of Trávinás.

Karnish: The mountain men of southeastern Vale who lived, rebelled and even ruled more or less autonomously for centuries without formal recognition by the Valen Throne. When the Twin Monarchy was established in 1254, the Tirion-Doreth Pact made the Karnish King the equal ruler of Vale. Karnish ancestry is believed linked in some way to the Horrand peoples. (See: Horrand)

Kathylón: Foremost of the Ferás-sûn settlements, deep in the heart of the forest in Highcrest.

Kiá: White-furred Ferás-sûn tribe dwelling in the tundras of Göurnoth. Their society depends upon following Cröd and Tragimi herds.

Knights of the Rapier: Predecessor organization of the Tirionus Elite. Initially dedicated to guerilla fighting in the time of Horrand occupation of Vale (1291–1293).

Kräga: The virtue-sworn warriors of Horrand society. Something like a cross between a knight and a roving barbarian, each Kräga dedicates their life to the pursuit of a single virtue, and allies only with Houses or authorities which uphold these.

K'ras Council: Noble governing body of Nazgan, populated by the Bordish Jeh'Mhár.

Lársólá: Language of the Aven people. Ancient and delicate, its syllabic structure and flowing, ornate script sets it apart from other tongues of the continent.

Leáthárá: The Ferás-sûn concept of absolute unity of the tribes (See: Wûlóká). A controversial concept, among the fractious Wolven people.

DEATH MASK

L'Intázá: Human nobles long residing in Karathis (see: Kara'Zin) and forming a council which prevailed upon the authority of the Valen regent who ruled the city for centuries. When the Bords conquered Karathis and renamed it to Kara'Zin, the LIntázá were initially allowed to remain, then finally deposed and replaced with the K'rás Council, ruled by the Jeh'Mhár.

Lóriális: Merchant and diplomatic caste of Aven society. Spurned among their own as "parasites," they are well connected among the other nations of Trávinás.

Lyndenál: Legendary land mass which hovers above the Aven Kingdoms. Site of the Academies of Lyndenál, only flighted, adult Aviári are permitted entry, and even then, only with sponsorship of a Lyndenáli lord.

Lyndenáli: Magick-suffused, politically-minded caste of the Aven peoples.

Lyntiá: "Lady of Life." Bride of Ánái, and one of the Driváni believed to be slumbering in the mysterious East.

Menuvia: Grand city in the mid-south region of Vale and former seat of the throne. After the fall of the Cerulean Empire, it was divested of its status and relegated to the site of the Valen Senate.

Menuvian: Peoples of the mid-southern region of Vale. Characterized by fairer skin, darker hair, and a connection of blood to Man's Aviári roots. A connection that their regional accent bears apparent evidence of.

Menuvian Republic Movement: A school of thought, or fomenting revolt, depending on whose interpretation one ascribes. Arising from the Menuvian senate, its advocates argue for the establishment of a Republic, and even a reformed Menuvian Military. (See: Bal-Ashid, Domus)

Mi'Mhád: Merchant Lords of Nazgan, uniting hundreds of guilds, and one of the most powerful branches of Nazgani government.

APPENDIX

Nát: (Izákás) Bordish word for Death.

Nazgan: (Izákás: "Land of Blood.") Westernmost continent of Trávinás. A windswept desert landscape inhabited primarily by the once-nomadic Bordish people. Its capital city is *Kara'Zin*.

NightVale: (Slang) Criminal shorthand for the underworld of Vale, and those who walk the "Shadowpath" (See: Shadowpath)

Pötho: "Justice." One of the Horrand virtues which the Kräga warriors swear their lives to.

Rávinás: Northernmost continent of Górn, and one of the more difficult to reach with present maritime technology. It has, however, been explored. And found inhabited by an unnamed, hostile reptilian race.

Relegant: King of Tirionus (1850–present) and among the older monarchs to ever take the throne.

Romatho: Northwesternmost village of Vale, almost bordering the nation of Nazgan. Agrarian by nature, its history has been marked by several "White Banner" peasant revolts, the most recent of which occurred in 1849.

Salár: The closest thing Nazgan has to a monarch. The Salár predates the Bords' conquest of Kara'Zin, their leadership proving invaluable during the Bords' nomadic years, beginning with Lord Linás'Ká (415–471) and extending to Lady Shi'Átás (1817–present). All branches of Nazgan government are subservient to the Salár.

Senate: Elite government body of Vale, populated by wealthy or connected Menuvian nobles and even a newly-ascendant dedicated political class. Though subservient to the Twin Monarchy, in recent years, it has come to fulfill a role more akin to a third pillar of its government.

Sensenal: Twin Capital of Vale, seat of the Karnish throne, and industrial heart of the nation lying at the feet of the Agrigör Mountains.

Shadowpath: The criminal creed of the "Wulf Pack," a now-defunct coterie of thieves and burglars based out of Menuvia. With their dissolution, the "Shadowpath" has become a sort of local legend, of "honorable" thievery in the name of squaring the scales of justice.

Shriá: Warrior tribe of the Ferás-sûn descended directly from Ántólás. (See: Wûlóká)

Sirvinás: (Easterlands) The scarcely-explored eastern continent discovered during the Age of Endeavor. Its discovery, and prospect of its exploitation presents a contentious dilemma, culturally and religiously, for so many faiths of the continent assert that the Driváni slumber on a nameless continent in the East.

Talorn: Official language of Vale and primary tongue of Men. Derived from the Lársólá language.

Thörg: House Lords of Göurnoth, who constantly vie for sole rulership of the snowy southern lands. (See: Firth)

Thörgen: "Loyalty," one of the virtues Kräga swear their blades to. Commonly associated with allegiance to a single House Lord. (See: Thörg)

Tirionus: Twin Capital of Vale, and seat of its political and financial power. Ruled by King Relegant (1850–present).

Torian: Seat of power for Men in the nation of Highcrest, and mediative influence between the Aviári and Ferás-sûn.

Tragimi: Swift bipedal, scaled creatures ideal for mountainous environments, hunted for their meat and hide. Domesticated as beasts of war and for messengers and scouting. Found in abundance in Göurnoth, Southern Highcrest, and southwestern Vale.

Trávinás: ("The Westerlands.") Western continent of Górn, and home of Vale, Göurnoth, Highcrest, and Nazgan.

APPENDIX

Tûnáni: Most worldly wandering tribe of Ferás-sûn, most commonly found in the river village of Tunwood.

Tunwood: Fishing village on the banks of the Virandia River in Highcrest.

Twin Kingdom: The joint rulership of the Tirionus and Sensenal crowns.

Tyrion: Primary currency of the Twin Kingdoms of Vale. Named after King Trivnius, also known as "Tirion" (1253–1270)

Underkingdoms: Rumored dwellings and trade routes of the "Delvers" of local legend. Carved deep beneath the powers of Trávinás.

Uplith: City lying to the west of Tirionus and northwest of Menuvia in the heart of Vale. Trading hub that unites the lower economic strata of Romatho with the higher-income heart of the Kingdom.

Vale: Easternmost nation of Trávinás and seat of the Twin Kingdom of Men. Its two capitals are Tirionus and Sensenal, uniting for the first time the Valen and Karnish crowns in a prolonged period of peace. It is bordered by Nazgan to the west, Highcrest to the North, and Göurnoth to the South. Its eastern coast touches the Sea of Cathmont.

Valen: Of the land or peoples of Vale. (See: Vale)

Válieri: Capital city of the Aven Empire in Highcrest, seat of the Aven Imperial throne.

Válieran: The monarchal caste of Aven society and keepers of its Imperial authority.

War of The Rift: (929–985) Largest enduring conflict in the history of Trávinás. Every government and people banded together to drive back a mysterious foe that appeared to have emerged from The Rift itself.

Warmaidens: House-sworn ladies of war in Göurnoth that first rose to defend their lords and homes from tyrant Firths in centuries past. Unlike the Kräga, their allegiance lies solely with family and Thörg. As Houses became more militarized, many warmaidens fell to mercenary work.

Westerlands: Valen common name for the continent of Trávinás. (See: Trávinás)

Whispering Windserpents: A breed of basilisk which emerged surprisingly recently in the deserts of Nazgan. Called such for the whispering hiss that seems invariably to herald their arrival.

White Banner Revolts: A series of revolts in the underclasses of Uplith and Romatho, the most recent of which concluded in 1849, predominantly preoccupied with workers' rights and a need for senatorial elections.

Wulf Pack: Notorious gang of thieves operating primarily in Menuvia, Blackcroft and Uplith under the leadership of the late Wulf Eghenston. Now defunct, after what appeared to be betrayal from within.

Wûlóká: Ferás-sûn tribes that form the basis for Wolven society. They number in the dozens, but the foremost among them are the Shriá, Kiá, Tûnáni, Viren, and Ákálár.

Xirfán: Oasis between Kara'Zin and Tralini, in the Modari region at the heart of Nazgan, making it a key trading hub.

Xy'Diás: Mountain range that spans the northwestern tip of Vale and stretches into the northeastern edge of Nazgan. The city of Romatho lies at its feet, with the Badlands and the Teeth of Nazgan lying beyond, to the north.

Zala: "Tin," a denomination of Nazgan currency.

Zhi'há: (Izákás) Bordish word for Narcotic.

Zi'Zin Temple: Foremost religious sect of Nazgan, representing the theocratic branch of the Nazgani government.

Xerdes will return!

Xerdes will continue to walk the shadowpath in new Nightvale adventures:

- *The Faceless Phantom*

- *Children of the Charnel House*

Also available:

- *Nightvale I—The Long Moonlight*

CPSIA information can be obtained
at www.ICGtesting.com
Printed in the USA
JSHW031728150223
37575JS00008B/16